Any Fool Can Be A Villager

By the same author

ANY FOOL CAN BE A COUNTRYMAN
(Pelham Books)
ANY FOOL CAN BE A PIG FARMER
(Farming Press)
ANY FOOL CAN BE A DAIRY FARMER
(Farming Press and Corgi)
THE DEVON BOOK
(Clover Press)
THE SOMERSET BOOK
(Clover Press)
THE AVON BOOK
(Clover Press)
THE CORNWALL BOOK
(Clover Press)

Any Fool Can Be A Villager

JAMES ROBERTSON

Illustrated by Larry

PELHAM BOOKS

LONDON

First published in Great Britain by
Pelham Books Ltd
44 Bedford Square
London WC1B 3DP
1984

British Library Cataloguing in Publication Data
Robertson, James, *1945–*
Any fool can be a villager.
1. Country life—England—West Country
2. West Country (England)—Social life and customs
I. Title
942.3′0858′0924 S522.G7

ISBN 0-07207-1544-X

Typeset by Cambrian Typesetters, Aldershot, Hants
Printed and bound by Billing & Sons Ltd, Worcester

Chapter One

A COUPLE of times in a decade, the British summer lets go all its inhibitions. It becomes bored with rationing out its sunshine during the short gaps that punctuate the watery march of the stately depressions sweeping in from the Atlantic and decides to have itself a heatwave. They are really quite respectable heatwaves when they come, with the thermometer climbing to levels that would not be considered untoward in places such as Cairo and Khartoum which sit and swelter under a tropical sun.

The Arab inhabitants of such places may be used to such climatic extravagance, but we are not. The fabric of our society starts to crumble in the face of prolonged sunshine. Water supplies run low. Fleet Street newspapers cannot find type large enough to headline the phenomenon. Trains run late as railway lines buckle while office workers copulate in the London parks at lunchtime. If such a heatwave should coincide with a Bank Holiday weekend, then there is a mighty national roar of agony as the British subject their pallid skins to a roasting that leaves them streaky with calamine lotion for a week.

The British landscape and those that dwell therein can stand this climatic extremism no better than its human inhabitants. Great heat takes the competitive edge out of the countryside. It saps the will. Cattle and sheep lie drowsily in the shade of hedgerow trees while farmers turn golden brown as they struggle with sweaty bales of hay. The summer birdsong stops as the land lies and cooks under the unwinking, moisture-sucking gaze of the sun.

They are good times, these. The drought may threaten the crops and the re-growth of grass but country people, like

everyone else, much prefer a good old-fashioned heatwave to the mingy insipid drizzle that is our summer norm.

Our village lay in a deep valley surrounded by steeply wooded hillsides. These did an excellent job of funnelling the storms of winter so that they released their furies on top of us and an even better job of trapping any drizzly cloud that may have been wandering past. The heat, for the villagers, was chiefly remarkable because of the increase in the area of naked flesh that the tourists felt obliged to reveal.

The men would put on their red nylon shorts with an effeminate slit up the side to reveal their pasty, office-white legs supported on open-toed-sandalled feet. There was a clear sex difference. In women tourists, the more beautiful the individual, the greater the quantity of unclothed skin she would reveal and the old patriarchs of the village would totter into the pub, wild-eyed with lust, full of talk of bulging breasts and firm nipples sheathed in filmy swathes of silk or cotton with sleek brown bellies beneath.

Contrarily, the fatter the man, the more he would show and one would see an absurdly thin couple of shanks transporting a great rippling, reddening roll of fat down the street while the owner sucked ice cream and gazed about him with mild incurious tourist eyes. They looked like giant tomatoes with a couple of cocktail sticks thrust into the base.

Curiously, a heatwave did not encourage tourists to paddle in the river which, as it entered the village, settled into a chain of quiet pools. Half a mile below the village lay the Long Pool, an idyllic stretch of water 200 yards long above a weir that had once powered a turbine supplying the first electricity to the settlement. Even on the hottest summer day this pool was usually deserted until the end of the afternoon when the local farmers and shopkeepers tottered across the field between the slumbering bullocks, peeled off their clothes and fell, like logs, into the water where they grampused around, splashing at the biting horseflies while they washed the day's dust and sweat from their bodies.

It would have taken only one weekend visitor or coach driver to light upon the pool and it would have been ruined when the hordes discovered its peace, forcing the owner of the stretch of water to wire it and erect notices to frighten away the trespassers. As long as the pool remained just the playground of the locals, he permitted it to remain as a private village amenity.

What may have helped to discourge the casual visitor was that the field next to the river was populated by a herd of extremely large cattle. The field was owned by the squire, an archetype of the old-fashioned courteous country gentleman, and in it he kept his herd of twenty or so Charolais cattle. They were huge white creatures with great trembling double-muscled buttocks crammed full of expensive and tender steaks. These animals were lorded over by a bull, a truly enormous beast that frightened away everyone who did not get close enough to see the mild contemplative expression in his big brown eyes – mirrors into a nature that possessed the inherent ferocity of a butterfly newly emerged from the chrysalis. You would walk past the whale-like bulk of this creature as he snoozed amid the buttercups and give him an affectionate slap on the backside. A few seconds later, the nerve impulse that the slap had generated might reach the animal's brain and he would open a sleepy eye, fringed by impossibly long eyelashes. It might even set his internal motor into gear and he would sweep his head round with the ponderous precision of the jib of a crane, to look benignly after you while a half-hundredweight of grass came rippling up his throat to be cudded between his enormous jaws.

This animal, appropriately named Snowflake, passed his days in total tranquillity save for the periods that he set aside for copulation. Then, one day, he decided to do something different. The heatwave had climbed to its peak and, deep down in the tortuous depths of Snowflake's brain, he must have become dimly aware that it was hot. He even managed to make the quantum leap in the quality of his thought by deciding that it lay within his competence to do something about it. Having achieved all that, Snowflake went downhill from then on. At some point during the heat of the day, he winched himself to his feet and ambled across the field towards the river.

He must have reached the bank, decided that the water looked cool and managed to find the one beach – about 5 feet in length – where he could wade in without having to brave a dive of a couple of yards down the sheer bank into the water. The weighty beast must have experienced a feeling of elation akin to that discovered by the first hippopotamus that ever ventured into a river when he found that the supermarket freezerful of meat tightly packed round his skeleton was transformed to the equivalent of thistledown by the buoying effect of the water. Snowflake plodded his way to the centre of the river and either waded or floated downstream to the very edge of the weir where the water was a fathom deep and there he rested with his chin laid comfortably on the concrete edge of the weir wall. He put his brain carefully back into neutral and closed his eyes in the blissful cool.

The workers of the village failed to turn up that evening for their usual dip because there was a needle cricket match taking place. This exceedingly coarse tournament between ourselves and the two villages that lay further down the valley was a regular occurrence every second Thursday in June and took precedence over even the hay harvest. Our village came in last as usual, but it meant that Snowflake was left undiscovered for twenty-four hours longer than might have been expected.

I was first down to the pool the following afternoon. Usually there would have been total silence except for the hum of insects and the occasional plop of a trout. On this occasion, the bellyflopping of these fishes was augmented by an eerie moaning noise.

Only those who know bulls can be aware of the remarkably unbull-like sounds that they are capable of making. Unlike in our own species, it is the cow's voice that breaks, while that of the bull tends to climb an octave with every passing year of his life. Snowflake was no dewy-eyed calf; he was a portly mature father of dozens of calves and he could have sung an operatic aria that would have rivalled Callas in her prime. His pure soprano, with just a touch of professional tremolo, was echoing off the water to bounce against the deep midsummer green of the trees. He was standing hock-deep on a ridge of rock by the weir, a long way from his only possible exit. The river at this point was about 25 yards wide and, although the bed was otherwise entirely flat, there was a raised rocky platform, which came to within 18 inches of the surface, that ran down its centre towards the weir. When he saw me coming, Snowflake loosed off another cadenza from his vantage point. There was a moment's hesitation while he tried to decide whether I was a potential saviour or an assassin who might be wielding a pole-axe or even a harpoon, and then he launched himself off his ridge towards me, sending a tsunami-sized wave boring up and down the length of the pool.

Had he been a sheep, or even an average-sized bullock, it would not have been too difficult to lean down the bank to grab a nose, an ear or a tail and given him that extra bit of impetus required to pop him up on to the bank. But he was Snowflake. I entered the water beside him and slapped his backside in the hope that it might encourage him to climb the bank. It was like slapping the boot of a family saloon and had much the same effect, except that the sound was a soggy splat rather than a beer-can 'ting'. I looked at Snowflake and he looked mournfully back at me.

I pulled at his ring and knew what aspiring kings must have felt before Arthur came along to pull out the sword. He shook his head, swinging me off my feet, and released one of his pure siren-like bellows. This was obviously a situation that was beyond my powers to correct and I decided that the squire would be quite interested to hear that a couple of thousand pounds' worth of his favourite bull was in danger of drowning itself.

I put my clothes back on and trudged the half mile or so to the call-box in the village. The squire was not answering his telephone. Following a local fashion the year before, he had dug himself a pond which he had stocked with trout and he tended to spend much of his time sitting in the middle of it in a rowing boat with a fishing line out and his toes dangling in the water to keep cool. I dropped into the post office to brief the post mistress who had the remarkable ability to transmit information, preferably scandalous, to the whole parish within a matter of hours. Some suspected that she used telepathy. Snowflake's popularity ensured that the nucleus of a decent posse was already gathering down by the bridge by the time I re-emerged.

Mary Mowbray had been visiting the saddler to gear herself up for the approaching hunting season. She was the wife of one of the nearby moorland farmers, Grenville, and was one of those thin, tough countrywomen who could have been any age from thirty to sixty. Her conversation was entirely horses, dogs and cattle. She had a couple of teenage children who seemed quite normal, although it was said that her lack of interest in them had meant that they had been unable to talk until they had first gone to school.

Trapped in the front seat of Mary's Land Rover and looking decidedly worried was fellow farmer Dennis. He, poor man, had been flagged down on his way from the big city where he had been visiting his wine merchant. This was a regularly monthly happening, during which he spent a pleasant afternoon trying to decide which brand of peaty malt whisky he should drink the following month. He consumed a case of the stuff every fortnight, so he was allowed a decent tasting session. As a result, it was doubtful whether Dennis would be in a condition to be particularly helpful during Snowflake's crisis.

Mary had also roped in Seth and Ishmael Matravers. They were brothers, now both in their late forties, who farmed in a desultory fashion on the edge of the parish as a cover for their shared passion for hunting. They looked remarkably alike, both being about 6 feet tall and weighing between 17 and 20 stone apiece, which necessitated the ownership of horses that shook the very earth as they passed. Their mother had been widowed early and the brothers had made her life a continual drudgery by leaving her to do all the farm work while they gadded about the moors and the countryside in pursuit of foxes and deer. On her demise, Mother had ensured her revenge with all the cunning of a Renaissance pope. The land she had bequeathed to Seth while the buildings, stock and machinery had gone to Ishmael, causing constant conflict between the weighty pair whose quarrels became legendary in the neighbourhood.

We all headed back down the lane in Mary's Land Rover and across the field to the river for the rescue of Snowflake. Nothing very much had changed since I had seen him last. He had moved across to the far bank and was browsing on the vegetation. As our vehicle bounced to a halt opposite him, he stopped chewing and turned to gaze at us with a sprig of meadowsweet dangling rakishly from the corner of his mouth. The Matravers stood up in the back of the Land Rover and assessed the situation.

'If we get a rope round his neck, we could haul him across and straight up the bank with the Land Rover,' said Seth.

'Don't be bloody silly,' replied Ishmael. 'It's a 5-foot bank and you'd either bugger up the clutch, spin the wheels or pull the beast's head off. The only way to get it out is to drive it back up the river to the beach.'

We disembarked, walked over to the bank and looked across at Snowflake. He gazed hopefully in our direction and sirened his encouragement without dropping his meadow-sweet.

'Won't do the fishing much good, this sort of thing,' said

Dennis, looking rather hot in his tweed suit. 'Whose is it?'

'The squire's of course,' replied Mary, lighting up one of the small cheroots that she carried in the handkerchief of her hacking jacket. She never took it off as she needed it to carry around the sugar lumps and peppermints that she fed to her horses.

'Really? I thought the squire had sold it about ten years ago.'

'It ain't ten years old yet,' replied Mary.

'Not the bull, the fishing.'

'Oh, the fishing. It must belong to the hotel.'

'In that case we'd better get the animal out as soon as possible before some clot of a holiday maker sticks his hook into it and claims it as his catch.' Dennis had a very low opinion of the quality of guest that frequented the nearby hotel to sample the various country sports that it laid on for its clientele. He was a member of a shooting syndicate in which the hotel leased a couple of guns and reckoned that he had been lucky to escape with only half a dozen pellets in his backside and a lightly wounded retriever the previous season. 'I suggest that some of us get into the river.'

'But we'll get wet,' objected Seth.

'That's very true,' said Ishmael and they both looked at me. I resignedly stripped off my outer garments and clambered back into the river with a rope. Under instruction from those on the bank, I waded across to Snowflake and draped it round his neck. I returned with the other end and climbed back on to the bank.

'Now what do we do?' I asked.

'We pull, of course,' said Dennis.

'I doubt if it will do much good.'

We lined up on the rope and, with Seth and Ishmael anchoring us at the back, we pulled. A hurt look crossed Snowflake's face as the rope rose, dripping, from the river and became tense. He tossed his head and the five of us who were pulling were scattered amid the thistles and cowpats.

Dennis regained his feet, swearing. 'I don't think that is going to get us very far. I think we need some more volunteers. Mary, go and see who you can dig up.'

Off went Mary and the rest of us settled on the bank to keep an eye on Snowflake. He shook himself, sending up waves, and turned back to the bank to nibble at some more meadowsweet. Seth and Ishmael each picked a daisy and chewed at the stem.

Colin, the hotel's water bailiff, was next to arrive, attracted by the sight of a vehicle in the field. He lived in terror of poachers stealing the hordes of sardine-sized trout that filled the river. He strode up the bank to where we sat. We placidly returned his gaze. It was rather restful, just sitting in the sunshine.

'What on earth are you lot up to?'

Seth picked a particularly succulent daisy and nodded towards the river. Colin looked and saw. 'Oh hell! I knew that was going to happen some day. Where's the squire?'

'Dunno,' said Seth. 'He's probably on his pond.'

'The old fool should have fenced off the river.'

'I don't see why,' objected Seth. 'You don't expect a beast to go into the water like that.'

'You can expect anything from a beast like that one. It always surprises me that it's got enough sense to impregnate its cows.'

'It's got enough sense to know how to get cool.'

'What's being done about it?' demanded Colin.

'Mary's gone to get some more help.'

We continued to sit in the sun and observe Snowflake. He was having a few problems. By browsing at the edge of the river, he was flushing out the horseflies that lurked beneath the trees for anything worthwhile which came their way, landing on their victim like thistledown before viciously sinking in their proboscises. Snowflake's aquatic environment left him at a grave disadvantage. He could twitch his mighty body in irritation but the highly effective fly swatter that was conveniently attached to his backside could not operate under water and he was forced to retreat to the ridge in the centre of the river, his bellow proving no defence against being bitten.

Mary returned bearing a heavy burden of local citizens. Half the shops in the village must have shut down to supply them. Straggling across the field after her came the first of the tourists who had begun to suspect that something interesting was going on downstream. Judging by the sounds that were issuing from their lips, they were the contents of a Glaswegian coach. They lined up on the bank, parting the willows, and gawped at Snowflake and the prone mounds of the Brothers Matravers.

Ishmael heaved his 18 stone up on his elbows and looked back at them, meditatively picking his nose. Most of the locals were as unselfconscious in front of the tourists as they were in front of their stock. I could never achieve this. I was once shown round a deep-litter chicken house by its proud owner. He had opened the door and walked in with myself following. The 5000 chickens that had been wandering round scratching at their dung had immediately frozen in their tracks and fixed us with their beady little eyes. I had found my hand straying nervously to my flies to make sure that they were properly done up.

Among the latest arrivals was another local farmer, Ivor. He was famous for getting things done and so he straight away took charge of the situation. He rousted us off our backsides.

'Right. I suggest we all get into the water and drive the bull back upstream to the beach where it'll get out by itself.'

There was a general mutter of complaint, but Ivor's assumption of compliance was too powerful to be gainsaid.

Ivor foolishly jumped off the bank while most were more circumspect. Snowflake was standing on his ridge in the middle in about 18 inches of water but, by the bank, the river was at its average depth of 5 feet 6 inches. Ivor was not built of the same mighty thews as the Brothers Matravers and he disappeared beneath the surface to come up, spluttering with indignation, to a round of applause from the gallery which was growing all the time. The local policeman, Percy, had joined the crowd but he was staying well in the background in case he was expected to strip off his uniform and jump in. It was known that his torso was brown – the brown of a policeman who parks his panda behind a convenient bush on a hot afternoon for a sunbathe rather than chase evil-doers and he was rather selfconscious about it.

Ivor positioned his troops on the rope. The Matravers took up their place at the back with myself and half a dozen others taking up the slack. Ivor stationed himself behind Snowflake and pulled his tail up over his back while half a dozen others found convenient handholds round his person. Snowflake did not seem unduly perturbed by this plethora of munchkins that were swarming round him, but he was rolling his eyes a bit at the mob of tourists on the bank. At Ivor's signal, we all took up the strain and heaved. It was one thing to pull the church choir off its feet at the village fete, but quite another to shift a motorcar-sized object with legs instead of wheels, especially whilst we were standing nipple-deep in water. Those in front pulled and those behind pushed while Snowflake, apparently pleased to have some purpose in life again, stood like the Rock of Ages and refused to co-operate.

Ivor paused to re-think his tactics. He untied the rope from Snowflake's neck and attached it to his ring instead. We repositioned ourselves and pulled. This was not quite such fun for the animal. His neck was thick enough to stand up to any force that we cared to apply, but not his comparatively delicate nostrils. He took an uncertain step forward as they stretched like a rubber band, while the audience hissed its disapproval at such wanton cruelty. Then his ring snapped, corroded by a couple of years of bovine snot, and to the delight of the spectators and to despairing cries from the river, all those on the rope disappeared beneath the water.

We all clambered back on to the bank to hold another

conference. The fire brigade turned up to join in the fun. They were a perfectly innocuous bunch of people normally – a mechanic, the cafe owner, an electrician and a couple of farm workers – but, once they put on their uniforms and climbed on to the back of their shiny red wagon, they seemed to think that they were capable of sorting out any problem short of the origin of the universe.

All the while the tourist hordes were thickening. There must have been nearly forty by this time, their customary slack-jawed gape at the passing pageant of life by now being replaced with a certain animation and other signs of humanity, while one or two of them even joined the experts in the water to see if they could help.

Snowflake looked magnificent, standing high on his ridge above the surface of the river with the crowd of mere humans partially submerged below him. Mick, ace tractor repairer and fire chief, stripped to his Y-fronts and took to the water to explore the river bed with his toes while Ivor went off to find another ring. To show his authority and station in life, Mick

kept on his white helmet and it was this that seemed, for the first time, to stir some emotion in Snowflake's broad breast.

As the helmet approached, he lowered his head and snorted with alarm before launching himself off his ridge and paddling down towards the weir. He had become well practised in aquatic locomotion in this depth of water and he moved surprisingly fast in a most unbovine series of undulating bounds. The multitude of rescuers, bathers and sightseers who by this time populated the river scattered before him like dinghies before the majestic advance of the royal yacht. Some failed to make it and were swamped by his bow wave, but most of them popped up again after he had passed and had come to rest about 30 yards further downstream with only his head now showing above water.

Colin, mindful of his fish, stood on the bank and wrung his hands. Mick joined him while a couple of tourist children on a plastic inflatable whale parked their vessel on Snowflake's back and he wriggled his appreciation as they leaned out and scratched him. Percy came to join the worried group of would-be rescuers.

'That bull doesn't look as if it wants to come out, if you ask me,' he said.

'Well, we didn't ask you, so shut up,' replied Colin.

Chapter Two

MATTERS IN the rescue of Snowflake had now reached a bit of a crisis. Ivor had decided not to go to look for a new ring in case something interesting happened while he was away and he was afraid that Mick might take over his position as *de facto* leader of events. He was prepared to consult, however.

'Have you any advice, Mick?' he asked.

Mick, still in his helmet and pants, gave the matter due thought. 'It's a bit of a problem. We can't haul him up the bank because it's too steep and it would need a vertical lift which we can't achieve. We can't get a winch into the river further up so that we could drag him back all the way to the beach, because there's no chance of getting the fire engine into the field, let alone into the river, and the brute is so strong that we can't drive him. Could we knock a hole in the weir and lead him through that?'

'No,' said Colin firmly. 'You'd muck up the flow of water to the trout hatchery and end up with half a million dead fish. In this heat they need all the water and all the oxygen they can get.'

'So that's out. How about getting a JCB to dig out the bank here to give him a way out?'

'It wouldn't work,' replied Ivor. 'There's solid rock only a foot beneath the surface. It would take dynamite to shift it.'

'Could we get a crane in?' suggested Seth.

Mick gave him a scornful look. 'We can't get our fire engine in without knocking down half a mile of hedge along the lane and the same would apply to a crane.'

There was an interested semi-circle of tourists listening-in to the discussion. One of them, a plump middle-aged lady in thick-lensed spectacles, tried to join in. 'Excuse me,' she said.

Mick looked at her in irritation. Civilians should be seen but not heard. Percy the policeman came into his own and began to wave his arms about as if he were driving chickens.

'Stand back. Would you please clear the bank. Come on, madam. Please step back.' He shooed them all back by about 10 yards to leave a clear demarcation space between the locals who thought they knew what they were doing and the tourists who had just come to watch. The experts continued their council of war.

'You know what I think?' said Mick.

'What?'

'I think that the only way we're going to get him out is to have him winched out from above.'

There was a stir of excitement from the rest of us.

'You don't mean . . . ?' queried Percy.

'He does mean,' said Seth.

'It's the only way,' said Mick firmly. 'We're going to have to call in the Brylcreem Boys.'

'Of course,' said Dennis, the residue of his tasting session making his brain work rather slower than the rest of us, 'a helicopter.'

The RAF is very much a part of last-resort agriculture, pelting blizzard-bound sheep with bales of hay, dropping toilet rolls on cut-off villages and doing all sorts of similar good works. If it did not issue such enormous bills for its services along with its bounty, it would have been used much more frequently. The glamour of ordering up a helicopter and its laconic crew of Biggles look-alikes appealed greatly to everybody and here was a situation where we could all enjoy the fun without being landed with the bill.

'What do you think, Ivor?' asked Mick.

'I think it's the only thing to do,' said Percy, interrupting the experts in his enthusiasm.

'Shut up, Percy,' said Mick.

'I think we'd better get in touch with the squire,' said Ivor. 'It could cost him a tidy penny or two, if they agree to come out.'

'Tell them that you'll sue them for disturbing your hens or something if they don't co-operate. Their bloody jets are always tooling round the spire of the church like a flock of bloody jackdaws,' said Ishmael.

This was an aspect of life in the valley to which newcomers took some time to grow accustomed. The valley, with the village and its church at the head, must have had a similar topography to one of the bombing runs to the Kremlin as young pilots, their acne clearly visible to observers on the ground, were continually hot-rodding up and down over the village. It was only disconcerting if one was in a car or on a tractor, when the sudden increase in engine noise as a jet scraped its belly along the top of the roof made one think that the vehicle was about to blow up.

'Talk of the devil,' said Dennis, as the squire's four-wheel-drive Subaru bounced through the gateway into the field and roared across the grass towards us, scattering tourists before it. He came to a stop and skidded in a cowpat as he emerged. The mirth from the tourists did nothing to improve his temper. He was wearing open-toed sandals underneath his Eighth Army-pattern khaki shorts.

'What the hell's this all about?' he snapped.

Ivor quickly apprised him of the situation and he strode to the edge of the bank to take stock. Snowflake was still up to his neck in water down by the weir and was licking a blue and white plastic dinghy containing a little girl who was squealing with delight.

'Hm. I see the difficulty. Can't we winch him upstream?'

'It would need a rope several hundred yards long to get him back to that little break in the bank and it would probably injure him,' replied Ivor.

'We certainly can't have that. I've just agreed to sell vast quantities of his semen. I had a chap out the other day who thought he was one of the best Charolais bulls in the country and the last thing I can afford is that any harm should come to him. Damned animal! He would go and get himself stuck now.'

Percy, his eyes gleaming with anticipation, chose his moment to sidle up. 'I think there's a way to get him out safely, Squire. It'll probably cost a bit, though.'

'Well, come out with it, man,' said the squire impatiently. 'I can't let the beast stay there all day. He's liable to exhaust himself and then drown.'

'The RAF.'

The squire turned pale. 'O God!' he said faintly. 'Has it come to that?'

'I'm afraid so,' replied Ivor.

The squire sighed heavily. 'If you're sure there's no other way, I suppose I'd better go and telephone them.'

'I'll come too,' said Dennis.

'So will I,' I offered.

'And me,' said Ivor.

'I'll keep the crowds back and clear a space for the helicopter,' announced Percy.

'We'll help,' said the Brothers Matravers.

'Excuse me,' said the plump lady in thick spectacles.

'I'm sorry, madam,' said Percy. 'You'll have to keep well back. We've got a helicopter coming in.'

Mary, who had been sitting on the bonnet of her Land Rover sucking peppermints and smoking her cheroots, suddenly came to life. 'What you could do, Squire, is charge some of these people who are coming along to watch. It might help to defray the cost of the operation.'

'That's a jolly good idea,' replied the squire, brightening up a little. 'Percy, would you mind handling that?'

The policeman looked justifiably outraged. 'I can't do that sort of thing. I'm a constable in uniform and it would be completely against the rules if I went round this lot with a hat.'

'I'll do it for 25 per cent of the take,' offered Seth.

'I'll do it for 20 per cent,' countered Ishmael.

'I'll do it for nothing, provided you give your usual Christmas party for me and the lads,' declared Mick. 'And you order the booze through me,' he added.

'How very kind of you,' said the squire. 'What I would suggest is that you charge . . . er . . . let's say 50p for adults and 25p for children. That sounds about right, wouldn't you agree?'

Leaving Mick and Percy in charge of matters by the river, the telephone party returned through the village in the

squire's car to the manor. The house was beginning to show evidence of a century's neglect but, on a hot summer day, the Virginia creeper and clematis that climbed all over the walls covered its blemishes and the interior no longer had the icy dankness that spoke of attempts to save on heating bills, but instead oozed a luxurious coolness.

The squire's wife was pottering in the garden like a character in an Edwardian play. She stopped deadheading the roses as we swept up the drive to park in front of the columned porch of the house and crossed over the lawn towards us, stripping off her gardening gloves as she approached. She wore a blue blouse and skirt with matching rope-soled sandals, the shade of which she had been crafty enough to match exactly with the vivid blue of her eyes that beaconed out of her tanned face. She was in late middle age and still stunningly beautiful; how the squire had won her was a bit of a mystery. She was even reputed to be rich.

'What's all the excitement about, dear?' she asked, as her husband leapt out of the car, galloped across the gravel and disappeared into the house.

'It's Snowflake. He's gone and got himself stuck in the river,' replied Dennis.

'Oh dear, the poor little chap.'

'We're going to phone for a helicopter to come and rescue him.'

'That sounds like a sensible idea. I do hope he won't be too frightened.'

'No,' said Dennis. 'I'm sure he will be all right.'

'Good,' she said. 'I must get back to the roses.' She drifted off as we turned towards the house, calling back over her shoulder, 'Make sure they don't put their wires too close to his balls.'

'I'll tell them to be careful,' said Dennis.

The squire was in the library whose shelves were filled with ancient bound copies of *Punch* and thrillers by Sapper and Dornford Yates, most of which had a fine white mould growing over them. The RAF took some time to reply after he had dialled the number: at least half the four-minute warning passed before he spoke.

'Hullo . . . good . . . I'd like to order a helicopter, please . . . I know you're not a minicab firm. You see, we have a crisis . . . No, we're not the coastguard. I'm a farmer. My bull is stuck in the river . . . No, I don't think it's a job for the navy . . . Yes, it was very droll.' The squire lifted his eyes to the ceiling. 'Oh good! How very kind. We can expect you in about three quarters of an hour, then. Thank you so much.' He hung up. 'They're coming out.'

'I think you forgot something,' said Ivor.

'Really? What?'

'You didn't tell them where to come.'

'Oh, good heavens! Nor I did.' He picked up the telephone and dialled through once more. 'Hullo . . . Yes, it's me again. I forgot to tell you where to come. Now the easiest way is to follow the motorway until you hit the A3321, then take the second left and carry on until you cross the river, then right for a dozen miles and you can't miss it . . . Map reference? I've no idea. Just follow my directions . . .' He gave an embarrassed whinny of laughter. 'Oh, I'm so sorry, I forgot you wouldn't be coming by road. Let me see now. I think the best thing to do would be for us to mark the spot and you just follow the river upstream until you see it . . . Weight of the bull? I suppose that is a good point. I haven't put him on the scales recently. At least a ton, I should think . . .'

'A ton and a half,' murmured Ivor.

'. . . Perhaps even a ton and a half. Can you manage that? . . . Good . . . er . . . One final thing. How much do you think it will cost? . . . Oh, I see. Goodbye, then.' He put down the receiver.

'How much did he say that it would cost?' I asked.

'He said it wasn't his department.'

'Not to worry,' comforted Ivor. 'It's probably covered by your insurance.'

Dennis, on his way out through the door, suddenly stopped and turned, his eyes lighting up like fairy lights. 'I've just had a marvellous idea. Why don't we get on to the television people and get them to come out. You could charge them a whacking great fee. Imagine the pretty pictures they would get of a huge white bull hauled out of the river by a rope dangling from a helicopter. It would appear on the national news. They could sell it in America. They'd make a fortune.'

'That's not bad,' said the squire. He gnawed at his Groucho Marx moustache for a couple of seconds. 'You don't think it might make me look a little silly? It is my bull and some might say that it was actually my fault that it got into the river in the first place.'

'Who cares?' said Dennis. 'Think of the money.'

The squire thought of the money. 'Right. You get back on the phone while the rest of us get back to the river and prepare things for the helicopter.'

We went back through the village which was strangely silent, considering that it was the height of the season. The shops were all shut and the coaches which were normally surrounded by milling tourists, terrified to venture too far away in case their bus left without them, stood empty and lonely in the car park. Their passengers were toiling in unaccustomed fashion down the hot, dusty lane towards the river between the high hedge banks lined with campion and willow herb.

The squire ploughed through the stragglers, his horn tooting importantly as befitted the owner of the centre of the attraction. There must have been nearly a hundred people standing amongst the thistles by this time. Most were lined up on the river bank, having broken down the lower branches on some of the trees so that they might have a better view. Snowflake was back on the ridge, placidly chewing his cud, with only a few children in the water to keep him company.

Percy shooed the crowd away from the centre of the field and a couple of lines of discarded shirts were laid out in the shape of a cross which he had had the initiative to place as a guide for the helicopter. Snowflake's harem was lying on the grass right at the far end of the field, content to keep well away from the excitement.

We hung around and waited. Mick's wife, Beryl, who owned the cafe, had turned up with several cartons of ice cream which had a ready sale amid the spectators. Then Dennis returned from his efforts to attract television coverage. He was not looking particularly happy.

'I can't understand it,' he reported. 'They didn't sound all that interested. They said they already had the story covered. But how on earth could that be, since we were the only ones who knew about it?' He was most apologetic about his failure and passed his ever-present flask of whisky round which, in the late afternoon heat, was not as welcome as Beryl's ice cream.

In another half-hour, the helicopter came clattering down the valley. The tourists 'oohed' and 'aahed' with excitement but the local inhabitants, both animal and human, showed little interest. We'd had the lot over the village – Tornadoes, Sikorskys, Gnats, Phantoms, Harriers and even the Hercules, thundering low enough to shake the fillings in your teeth. The best of them had been the old Vulcan bomber. However many times we had seen it, it was still an event when its enormous triangular slab-shape slipped over the top of a hill and rumbled down the valley, spraying burnt kerosene out of its backside.

The helicopter chuntered up the river, stopped to examine Snowflake in a rather predatory fashion from 100 feet or so while he continued his cudding and then came over the field, causing the tourists to shriek with excitement, and settled on the grass, blowing all the shirts into the hedgerow. The blades slowly whumped to a stop and a door in its side opened. The crowd pressed forward. One almost expected a creature with a dozen tentacles to emerge and say, 'Take me to your leader.'

The behelmeted aristocrats who stepped out in its stead had a glamour that no extra-terrestrial could possess, however. These were not the spotty passers-by in the jet trainers, but the heroes who plucked bulls from rivers and small children off inflatables that were blown out to sea while their parents were copulating in the sand dunes. Their leader took off his helmet and came over to Percy who was standing beside the squire and other leaders of the community: 'That's the cow you want hauled out, is it?'

Mary sighed in appreciation. His hair was fair, his eyes were blue, his chin was firm, his nose was chiselled with a delicate flare to his nostrils and a scraggy blond moustache squatted on his upper lip. His accent was pure Scouse. 'My name is McKenna, Flight-Lieutenant McKenna.'

'Good afternoon, Flight-Lieutenant,' said the squire. 'Yes, that is the . . . er . . . bull . . . er . . .'

Dennis took over the socializing. 'Would you like a whisky?' he asked, proffering his flask. Then: 'Perhaps you'd prefer an ice cream,' he continued hurriedly as he received a basilisk stare from the pilot.

'Is your bull in any immediate danger?'

'No,' replied the squire. 'It's just that we can't get him out.'

'In that case, have you got a strawberry split? I do like a nice strawberry split.'

'Beryl! Have you got any strawberry splits?'

Beryl, a large lady, waddled over with her ice creams. 'Only one, Squire.'

'Not to worry,' said the pilot. 'I'll take that and I'll have a couple of chocolate flake cones for the lads.'

The crowd watched with grave interest as Beryl handed out the ice creams while looking expectantly at the squire. He sighed and fumbled in the pocket of his shorts, producing a crumpled fiver which she took and carefully counted out three notes in change.

'Is that all I get?' asked the squire.

Beryl looked hurt. 'I had the extra expense of transporting the ice cream from the village and putting it in the cold box. We've got to make a living.'

'Have you paid for the ice-cream concession in this field?' asked Dennis.

'A very good point,' said the squire and snatched another pound note from Beryl's grasp. We stood and watched the three-man crew as they sat in the shade of their machine, supping their ice creams. They finished them and showed little inclination to do anything else. The tourists moved in and started to poke the large yellow helicopter with 'RAF RESCUE' painted prominently on its side.

'When do you think they're going to do something?' asked Mary from the bonnet of her Land Rover. 'I can't sit here all day. I've got horses to feed.'

'When they're ready, I suppose,' replied Dennis.

'Do you think they charge by the hour?' she asked.

'Heavens!' said the squire. 'What a ghastly thought! Perhaps I'd better go and find out.' He advanced to the helicopter and had a short exchange of views with the flight-lieutenant. He returned to the Land Rover. 'He says they shouldn't be long now.'

We waited for another ten minutes.

'Look!' said Dennis suddenly. 'The rotten swine!'

A couple of Volvo estate cars had drawn up in the gateway of the field and a posse of people was coming through. It was a television crew. The RAF had spotted it as well and stood up and stretched. One of the TV people pushed his way through the tourists, went up to the pilot and shook his hand.

'Afternoon, Allan. Good of you to wait for us. This looks like being quite a goody. Let's have a look at the cow.' They went over to the river bank with the tourists trailing after them.

'Oh yes, this should make the network all right. Lovely creamy-white cow.'

'Bull,' snorted the squire, who was pushing his way through the mob after them.

'Bull, even better, dangling on the end of a cable. You'll have to pull it up slowly to make sure that we get some decent shots.'

The squire finally managed to make his presence felt. 'Here, we phoned you up and you said that you weren't interested.'

'It's all right, mate. We'd already been tipped off by the RAF.'

'What a damned cheek! It's my bull.'

'Is it? Oh well, we'll take an interview with you later. But it's great stuff for the RAF. Lovely PR. The taxpayers will think they're marvellous.'

The squire had an extremely short fuse at the best of times and a tidal wave of blood swept up his cheeks. 'This is nothing short of outrageous. I'm going to get a damn great bill while you people are going to make money out of it.'

'No need to get your knickers in a twist, my son. Remember that freedom of the Press is the corner-stone of our liberty.'

'I do not consider that a bunch of bloody nancy-boys with television cameras have anything to do with Press freedom.' Before the squire let the conditioning of a century of democracy fall away from him and grabbed Mary's horse-whip, Dennis took hold of his arm and whispered in his ear. The squire brightened. 'Good point, Dennis.' He turned to the director. 'Excuse me. Have you been given permission to film in this field?'

The director looked furtive. 'Don't need it.'

'I'm afraid you do.'

'All right, then, who do I ask?'

'Me.'

'Oh, I see. Well, may I have permission, then?'

'Certainly,' replied the squire with relish. 'It'll cost you . . . er . . .' Dennis whispered in his ear. '. . . £150.'

'£150! Bloody hell. We're News, not Features. That sort of

money would cover me for a week. How about a tenner?'

'I'm sorry,' said the squire firmly. 'If you want to film, it's £150 or nothing.'

The flight-lieutenant was fiddling uneasily with his helmet. The director looked appealingly at him, but he shrugged. This was not the sort of thing that had been covered during lectures at Cranwell.

'Come on, mate. We've driven a hell of a long way for this. It'll make you famous. Be a pal. Make it twenty quid,' pleaded the media man.

'£150,' said the squire.

The director took a deep breath. 'Right. Be like that. Charlie!' The cameraman, to whom this call was addressed, appeared to be totally uninterested in the outcome of the negotiations: he was much keener on exploiting his televisual glamour by allowing the most attractive female tourist in the field to peer through the viewfinder of his camera while he clasped her and it in his great hairy arms. 'Charlie! Do you think you could climb on to the top of the car and get decent

pictures from the next field?' The next field was only 100 yards away but there was the lane and the two 6-foot hedges bordering it in between.

Charlie raised his eyes from the tourist's cleavage and looked over at the hedges. 'Yeah, Ray. No problem.'

'Right then,' said Ray. 'We'll do that.'

'Excuse me,' said the squire. 'Have you got permission to use that field?'

'Don't tell me. You own that damned field as well.'

'That's right.'

Ray sighed heavily. 'Why are you being so difficult? Most people like to see themselves on TV.'

'For a start, Sir, I do not possess a television receiver and, in the second place, I am trying to offset the expense of that machine.' He flapped his hand in the direction of the helicopter.

'I suppose that's reasonable. Look. What I'll do is go and phone the editor and see if he will authorize £150.'

Meanwhile the tourists pressed closer to the helicopter and peered into its interior. Beryl re-appeared with a fresh load of ice cream and did a roaring trade. The Brothers Matravers tried to persuade the helicopter pilot to give them a joy-ride over their farm. Snowflake was, for the moment, ignored, while his cows, with the middle-aged female tourist amongst them, cropped their way up the river bank past him, most of them taking no notice of his plaintive cries of indignation.

Eventually Ray returned bearing good news. He prised the cameraman away from the brown-bellied nymph, who was now being taught the delights of zoom, pan and tilt, and came over to the squire: 'OK, you can have your money. But you'll have to send in an invoice for it. I can't produce that sort of amount from petty cash.'

His announcement was greeted by a ripple of applause from the tourists who had been afraid that they were about to be cheated of their spectacle and a chance of appearing on TV. A circle was formed round the protagonists in the drama about to unfold so that none of its nuances would be lost.

There was, however, a problem.

'Where's the bloody cow?' asked Ray, scanning the water.

'He hasn't drowned, has he?' asked the squire anxiously.

Snowflake hadn't drowned. He was 200 yards upriver and, as we watched in dismay, he pulled himself out of the water via the beach and mounted one of his harem.

'I thought that would happen,' said the middle-aged lady tourist. 'I saw that one of the cows was on heat and I drove her down the bank so that he could get a sniff of her and he followed like a lamb.'

The squire refused an additional £100 to push Snowflake back in. The RAF clattered away muttering about large bills and wasting their time but, as Dennis remarked, it was their own fault for hanging about when they first came. Beryl bought Snowflake a new ring out of her ice-cream profits and, for the first time in ten years, the TV station refused to announce the village fete on their future events programme. As the squire said, none of their employees was a gentleman, so we were not surprised.

Chapter Three

'TOURISTS,' SAID Arthur firmly. 'That's what I'm after. It's ridiculous to farm in an area like this and not make full use of the natural resources. Tourists are an annual cash crop like any other, and I'm going too make sure that I get my share of the harvest.'

Arthur, in the opinion of the locals, could hardly be said to farm in the area. He was a foreigner, having only lived in the vicinity for twenty years, and had come down from 'up country', a legendary region that took in all the land surface of the United Kingdom lying east and north of the county boundary. Arthur had begun his career as a relief milker, a locum for dairy farmers who had finally cracked under the strain of milking cows twice a day for year after year and had taken their wives for a fortnight's holiday to wander the sea front at Torquay at 5.00 am, worrying themselves to ulcers about what might be going wrong back home.

Arthur was quite good at his job and had been given a lot of work, but a *frisson* of horror had passed through the community when, after five years, he had gone out and bought a 50-acre farm. The farmers who had employed him all counted their cows, checked their silver spoons and did their inventories, but no discrepancies could be found. It was a baffling problem. Arthur, when approached directly about the source of his wealth, tapped the side of his long nose and winked. It was a gesture which looked impressive but was not very informative.

Percy's predecessor was even stirred sufficiently to make a few enquiries, but Arthur sent him off with a flea in his ear. Eventually it was agreed that Arthur was the son of a rich northern landowner and had had the money passed to him by his parent. This was totally imaginary but, by that stage, nobody cared. Every problem has to have its solution and any solution, however unlikely, was better than none.

Arthur's 50 acres were pretty useless. His financial cornucopia seemed to have stopped cornucoping before he was able to invest the large sum needed to drain and re-seed the muddy, rushy hilltop that he had purchased. It was the bogs that were his main problem. The water seemed to defy both logic and gravity by ignoring all the valleys that surrounded his farm belonging to other people and settled on the top of his mountain, refusing to move. Serious farming was not possible and he was forced into the ultimate agricultural cop-out of covering his land with sheep.

With his status raised from that of agricultural odd-job man to farmer, if only a sheep farmer, Arthur could no longer work for other people and so he built up a very reasonable business selling the sort of knick-knacks that farmers always need – concoctions to pour down animals' throats to drown worms, curious tools to help build barbed-wire fences and subtly curved knives with which to pare cows' toenails. But it niggled. There he was, a fully-fledged farmer, messing about with a few bone-headed sheep that needed gumboots if they were to thrive. Even all those cabinet ministers with their farms in the home counties kept beef as well as sheep.

'Tourists. It's got to be tourists,' he reiterated to the evening assembly in the pub. Of the two bars in the thatched building, the one with the nicotine-coloured walls and dung from muddy boots covering the carpet in a protective layer was used almost entirely by local inhabitants. Tourists used the lounge bar, complete with juke box and padded benches. Even though Arthur was a foreigner, he used the locals' bar.

'Tourists are supposed to like unspoilt countryside and nobody could call my land spoiled.'

'Well, I don't know about that,' said Bill. 'It's pretty spoilt-looking to me with all those weeds and rushes all over it.'

'No, you daft old pillock. That's unspoilt. The more useless and like a rubbish tip the land is, the more unspoilt it's supposed to be if you are a townsman. They all love weeds and nothing upsets them more if you go and turn a bit of barren land into a decent field of grass or corn. They've got laws against that sort of thing these days.'

'They're all potty if you ask me. They've no right to interfere with what a man does with his own land,' said Bill.

There were jeers from round the bar.

'Where the hell have you been for the last thirty years?' asked Arthur. 'Anyone would think you thought we still lived in a free country.'

'It's still not right,' grumbled Bill. 'They ought to stop people in towns digging up their vegetable gardens or mowing their lawns rather than come out and interfere with us farmers trying to make an honest living.'

That was rich coming from Bill. He was a farmer – or certainly had been – but he had not felt the need of restricting himself to making an honest living during any of his sixty-five years. It was not his fault that his bullocks always seemed to escape and find their way back home after he had sold them, or that his sheep spent most of their lives eating his neighbours' grass, or even if the driver of the milk tanker always seemed to be his wife's cousin which meant that the reading of the contents of Bill's bulk milk tank was always more than generous. It may not have been his fault, but it all helped to keep him in beer, baccy and racehorses.

Bill had been as bald as a mushroom for thirty years, but few people knew it as he never took off his trilby. It was rumoured that he kept a fighting fund of £20 notes inside, in case a sudden deal should come his way, but this theory was discounted by the more knowledgeable villagers because we knew, however sweet the deal, Bill would never remove his hat. I had once walked with him under an overhanging branch which had momentarily dislodged his head cover. Bill's sight of my startled look at the colour contrast between the smooth white toadbelly of his scalp and his gnarled, sun-beaten face, had made him blush deeply.

'Anyway,' continued Bill, 'not even the tourists would find any reason to visit your farm, Arthur. Why should they?'

'Bed and breakfast?'

'Bed and breakfast,' repeated Bill derisively. 'You won't

catch any tourists coming if they have to queue up for your outside khasi.'

'Oh, I don't know. It's the only double-seater in working order in the parish. It'd give them the authentic feel of country living.'

'Sure. An arse full of splinters.'

'You're an ignorant pig, Bill Hockridge,' broke in Arthur's wife, Annie. 'The seats are polished smooth by generations of backsides. You'd never get a splinter from them.'

'It's a hell of a thought, really,' said the commander, who ran a market garden on the edge of the village. Its profits, combined with his pension, just managed to keep pace with his alcohol consumption. 'Those seats must have cradled more than a century of bums. They must have watched little ones perch precariously on their edge as nippers, seen them grow into adolescence and get spotty before changing into the fighting trim of maturity, the flabbiness of middle age and then shrinking again as they move towards senescence. They could tell a tale or two about the frailty of human hopes and ambitions, those bog seats.'

The commander sometimes got like this with a few drinks under his belt.

'That's true enough,' said Bill. 'They've seen some important backsides too. The minister of agriculture's, for one.'

'The present one?' asked Arthur.

'No, during the war. A whole bunch of bigwigs came down with a newsreel team to make a film about how important farmers were to the war effort. The old squire gave them a meal in the manor and the whole lot of them got the trots. They went round to your place and they were bloody grateful that it was a double-seater. They didn't have to queue so long.'

There was a rapid series of clicks from a chair at the side of the bar which meant that Jimmy, the village's oldest inhabitant, was loosening his false teeth in order to make a pronouncement. We turned in anticipation.

'That privy must have known Maisie Appleyard,' he said. There was a reverent silence round the bar.

'Who's Maisie Appleyard?' I asked.

Bill answered, 'She was the most beautiful girl that was ever bred in the parish —'

'— and a real hard worker,' broke in Jimmy.

'She was that, too,' agreed Bill. 'She married a Yank during the war when she got pregnant. She was the only one who managed it. To marry a Yank.'

'Well, I suppose she had to if she got pregnant,' said Arthur.

'What do you mean, "had to"?' said Bill scornfully. 'I should think half the people in the parish have got an American parent or grandparent if they only knew it. All the girls were after one of those Yanks who were stationed in the house the commune's got now. They said they were training to be commandos but it turned out they were all casualties from what they called battle fatigue. We called the place the chicken house, and they sure behaved like roosters when they got the chance.'

'But they spent money in the village and we were grateful enough for that,' said Jimmy. 'All the shopkeepers changed the price tickets when they heard the American jeeps coming down the valley.'

'It sounds as if they were a bit like today's tourists,' said Arthur.

'They weren't the same at all,' answered Bill. 'The tourists just come down in their caravans and sit on the sites cooking up tins of baked beans they bought in Birmingham before they set out. They don't spend anything at all.'

'A caravan site!' said Arthur. 'That's what I'll do. We'll start up a caravan site.'

And he did. He made a grand job of it in one of his less boggy fields. He put down lorry-loads of quarry waste to make hard stands, dug a pit in which they could empty their chemical loos, put in a water standpipe – spring-fed from a bog in the field above – and erected a large sign by his front gate which announced that he was now open for business. It was even rumoured that he had applied for planning permission.

All the same, Arthur did not look a particularly happy man when he came into the pub a couple of months later. He ordered his usual pint, specifying a glass with a handle, which was one of those little foreign habits that he still retained, and gazed rather sadly down into his beer. Arthur, looking as if life was a bit of a desert drear, was an unusual and interesting sight and he was soon surrounded by a commiserating group of villagers trying to get him to talk. He was well into his second pint before he was willing to unburden himself.

'Bastards! That's what they are. A miserable crowd of bastards. I go and spend hundreds of pounds on a really lovely caravan site and nobody turns up. It's a waste of bloody time.'

'You know what's wrong with it, don't you?' said Bill. 'It's got no shelter. Sitting on top of your blooming hill, even the caravanners have got enough sense to know that they'd be blown into the next county if they went and parked there.'

'It's got views, magnificent views, for miles. That's what makes it special,' replied Arthur defensively. 'And you can't have both views and shelter. Either you're down in a valley or boxed in by trees where the weather can't get at you, or you're out in the open where it's windy and you can see a long way. Anyway, tourists are supposed to come out here to get lots of clean country air.'

'Not as much air as you're offering, Arthur. What are you going to do?'

'I don't know.'

'You ought to advertise,' said the commander. 'It's not as if you're on the beaten track.'

'I can't afford to. I spent all my money on preparing the site.'

'How about a bit of public relations, then?'

'What do you mean?'

'It's pretty much the same as advertising, but it doesn't cost you anything. You get newspapers to print stories about you and your caravan site,' replied the commander.

'Why should they want to do that?'

'You make the stories interesting.'

Arthur thought for a few seconds. 'How many interesting stories can you think of about a caravan site?'

'Well . . . I see what you mean. Can't you have a vicar in

a love nest with a verger's wife? That would get you mentioned in the mucky papers for a start.'

'It would, but I haven't had any caravans yet and, even if one did turn up, it would be highly unlikely to contain a vicar and a verger's wife.'

'You don't understand,' replied the commander patiently. 'In public relations you make up the stories. They don't have to be true. And, for heaven's sake, you don't expect to read true stories in the mucky papers.'

'I suppose not . . . You mean I can make up anything I like?'

'That's right.'

'Like what?'

'Well, let's think about it.'

And think about it we did. The campaign to put Arthur's caravan site firmly on the map was born that evening. If Arthur himself had known what he was getting into, the campaign would have probably been still-born, but he could have only reached that conclusion with the advantage of hindsight. We came up with the outline of a plan which was approved by all those present in the pub and we were all sworn to secrecy.

The following day, Bill, myself and Bill's elderly and extremely fat labrador went out to see Arthur and inspect the terrain. His farm was pretty bleak even when it was not too windy, though the house itself nestled into a bank which gave it some protection against the elements. Photographed from a distance, in soft focus, through a filter, it could have sold calendars by the thousand – white-washed under a thatched roof with a pond at its front and a stream running alongside. Close to, the illusion lost its potency. The pond was muddy and had once been described by a visitor from the water authority as being 'dangerously feculent', which was probably the fault of the ducks. There were a few fertilizer bags floating in the cocoa-coloured water and the long-dead corpse of a sheep.

Arthur's house was beginning to revert to the earth whence it had sprung, which became evident when we were asked in for a cup of coffee. Our host was one of that common breed of countrymen who begrudge spending any money on themselves or their dwellings and, less commonly, his wife appeared to be of the same persuasion. It is this habit which makes it so difficult for urban man to gauge the wealth of a countryman with any hope of accuracy. Some of the dingiest and least prepossessing individuals are those before whom the Stock Exchange would do well to tremble.

The farmhouse was dark with no windows on its bank side and small square portholes piercing the thick cob walls on to the duckpond. It was not possible to see through them, the glass being distorted by the passing of the years and obscured by a layer of grime and fly droppings. At one end of the house was the sitting room, the end wall of which was taken up by a cavernous fireplace still containing the original crucks on which the cooking pots would have been suspended a century earlier. The walls, whatever their original colour may have been, were grey – the dense grey formed by decades of smoke trying to force its way up through a chimney jammed with old jackdaws' nests before giving up to wreathe miserably round the room and settle there unfulfilled.

The dwelling had that unique, still, dead cold that can only be found in an unheated thatched building where the superb insulating qualities of the roof retain all the mould, must and damp from year to year. Arthur's thatch had actually passed the point of no return as much of it had decayed to slime and was letting in the rain to encourage a fine crop of mushrooms on the walls. Cob will last for ever, they say, provided it has dry feet and a dry head. The head of this house was now damp and it was surely only a matter of months before the walls began to slip away.

We sat in the kitchen, surrounded by sneezing cats and silver trophies won at gymkhanas by his wife, and discussed our PR campaign. We then repaired to the field where the caravans were supposed to be congregating and watched critically while Arthur erected a rickety wooden arch above the gateway and suspended a board on some baler twine from its apex. The board had 'Moorview Caravan Park', together with his address and telephone number, painted on it.

Bill instructed us to carry a few shovelfuls of mud from the ditch to add to the accumulation that already squelched in the gateway. He then carefully smoothed over the surface of the mud and summoned his dog which had been following these actions with a dubious expression on her face. The animal came, dragging her belly along the grass, and Bill forced her across the patch of mud. He examined the result, clicked his tongue in irritation, smoothed over the paw marks and tried again. This time he was satisfied.

The local paper came out the following Tuesday. There was a good splash. A picture across several columns showed Arthur standing in front of his sign above a large headline: 'LOCAL FARMER FINDS TRACKS IN FIELD – Threat to sheep in area'. Underneath was a lovely story. The tracks were thought to be those of a large black cat-like animal, according to the experts (Bill), and it did not seem to be thought strange that the animal's colour could be deduced from its footmarks. This theory was given further credence since the creature had been sighted by a retired vicar or verger who had been staying at the beautiful caravan site, with running water and hard

stands, at the time. According to Arthur, this man of the cloth said that he had been woken by some animal breathing heavily in the night just outside his caravan. With considerable courage, he had opened the door and had received a confused impression of a large, dark, cat-like animal, flashing white teeth and a sinuous shape. No, it had not been Eartha Kitt.

Like all truly great public relations exercises, the story took on a life of its own. The next stage after the arrival of the local newspaper was the appearance of a reporter from the neighbourhood's radio station. He caught Arthur unawares as he had been busy processing two caravans that had been directed to his farm by a garage on the main road. Arthur shuffled his feet a bit but cantered through his hollow tale about footmarks and vicars who had failed to leave a forwarding address and was told that, all things being equal, the interview should be broadcast at lunch-time on Sunday in a magazine programme.

There was a radio in the pub and most of those in the know turned up to listen to it. We were feeling pretty proud of ourselves. The media coverage was already greater than we had expected and Arthur was already welcoming caravans whose inhabitants had come puma spotting.

Perhaps it could be said that the reporter had gone a little over the top. 'Fear stalks the peaceful countryside,' he intoned, 'as a mysterious and ferocious beast terrorizes farmers and ravages sheep.'

'Ravages sheep?' said the commander. 'We said nothing about ravaging sheep.'

Arthur was trotted out to say his piece, but the star of the item was one of his neighbours, Frank Mattock. He was not a party to the original plot, but he had never been a slouch when it came to turning circumstances to his own advantage. Frank had recently invested in large numbers of sheep as an addition to his highly profitable dairy herd, but he had a brother-in-law who was an insurance salesman, a terrible burden for any man to bear. Farmers are very vulnerable to the predatory excursions of such bandits as the risks to which a farmer is liable are legion, from cows being killed by lightning, to foot-and-mouth, to spontaneous combustion in hay and even to rape and pillage by one's bull or ram amid the neighbour's stock.

Frank had had a little too much to drink a few weeks earlier in his brother-in-law's company and had woken up in the morning to find that he was the owner of a policy which covered him in the event of unnatural death in his sheep, with the Transglobal Insurance Company based in the Cayman Islands. It cost a fortune as sheep are peculiarly prone to unnatural death. After some thought, Frank put in a claim for a bunch of sheep that he was sending to the abattoir, deciding, perfectly reasonably, that their death could hardly be described as natural.

He was just stirring a bit and, if the insurance company had shown any signs of a sense of humour, all would have been well. But bureaucrats are bureaucrats and they all find money a desperately serious business. They appreciated Frank's claim about as much as a feminist convention would appreciate a flasher. Letters of remarkable acrimony went back and forth and they tried to cancel Frank's policy, but they were damned if they would refund his premium.

Frank sensed an opportunity to fight back. The speaker of the radio tied itself in knots to achieve a faithful rendition of his rural accent. No, he had not actually seen this puma, but he had seen tracks and had lost at least a dozen lambs with their throats torn out, an unnatural and untimely end.

'How did you know that the killer was a puma?' asked the reporter.

'I've lived in the countryside, man and boy, for forty-two years and this sort of damage is only caused by pumas.'

'Can you afford this sort of loss?'

'Fortunately, unlike many farmers, I am insured. But it's got to stop. The sooner this ferocious beast is killed, the sooner we can all get back to proper farming again.'

'Will it be difficult to kill? One would think an animal like this would find it very difficult to hide itself.'

'Not really,' said Frank. 'It could disappear into the woods and copses and never be found. I stayed up for three nights on the trot last week and never even saw the beast.'

'And did you lose any animals?'

'Yes, we had four lambs die . . . sorry . . . killed and we never heard a thing.'

The reporter moved on to a potted history of pumas from the well-known Surrey strain to a Welsh manifestation a year or two before and closed with a 'watch this space' type of announcement to ensure that his next piece on the subject would be broadcast. The pub was well satisfied. The puma was coasting along nicely and it looked as though Arthur's caravan site would receive plenty of new customers.

The puma really began to take off the following week. Other farmers in neighbouring parishes suddenly found that the animal was taking their stock. It received publicity in the local morning paper and was then discovered by Fleet Street. We watched in awe as it grew in fame and ferocity. It killed a pony and ate it all so that not a trace was left. The pub began to talk about its latest exploits in whispers as one could never quite be sure who was in the bar. There were strangers about wearing camouflage jackets, stout boots and binoculars with clear-eyed, white-hunter-type expressions. They tended to grip your arm as you passed and engage you in earnest conversation about likely puma habitats.

One of them lectured to us one evening in the pub. A woman of middling years who claimed to be the nation's leading authority on British great cats, she told us of the time that not one but *two* lions appeared in the north of England before a lay preacher who was walking down a country lane in deep conversation with a commissioner of oaths. The beasts were grinning at them from the shelter of a bramble bush. They reported the matter to the police who, as they had to do on such occasions, scoured the countryside with sharpshooters, only to discover that the animals had vanished into thin air.

All in all, it appeared that the wild British great cat was a very shy animal. They were almost always pumas and the only fully authenticated sighting was in Scotland where the creature could hardly be overlooked since its body was found. It turned out to have been stuffed and was thought to be a hoax. We clicked our tongues in disapproval at this. It was a peculiarity of the British puma that it always seemed to be black although the normal colour was sandy brown.

'Perhaps its coloration is due to the vagaries of the British climate,' I hazarded.

'That is certainly one possibility,' she agreed. 'However, the theory which I favour is that the British puma is a separate species which became isolated after the last Ice Age and a few of them have managed to hang on and breed in the remoter parts of the country.'

'Like Surrey,' murmured the commander.

'The particular animal we have here is almost certainly a female with a litter of cubs.'

'How on earth do you know that?' inquired the commander curiously.

'I've seen her and I know where her den is.'

There was a stunned silence round the bar. 'Where exactly was this?' asked the commander.

The expert gave a mysterious smile. 'I'm sorry, but I am

unable to tell you. If I said where it was, it would be shot. I intend to photograph it.'

'I see. Have you photographed other pumas?'

'Not exactly. But look at these. This is the Welsh puma.' The expert produced her snaps. They were not of the puma itself, since the British species only appears in the flesh on foggy days before people whose cameras have just run out of film, but of puma tracks. Her prize shot produced a hot debate.

'That's a fox,' said Jimmy, who had been a professional rabbit catcher in his prime and knew about that sort of thing.

'Nonsense,' said the commander. 'It's a dog.'

The expert started to huff and puff with indignation.

'It's a vixen. As sure as I've got eyes in my head,' insisted Jimmy.

'It's far too broad in the pad,' said Bill decisively. The expert perked up a bit.

'Course it's a fox,' said Jimmy.

'Never,' asserted Bill. 'I've seen enough fox tracks round my pheasant pens to tell the difference between a fox and a dog and this is a dog if ever I saw one. It's a big dog, mind, something like a foxhound or . . .'

'A labrador?' asked the commander innocently. Bill looked rather shifty and the expert broke in indignantly.

'How dare you say it's a fox or a dog. It's a puma. It's as plain as a pikestaff.'

'Look, Missus,' said Bill patiently, 'the difference between the track of a dog and a cat is that a cat always retracts its claws when it's walking and a dog can't. So if you can see the indentation of a claw in front of each toe, then you know what you're looking at has to be the pug mark of a member of the dog family. And this photograph has not only got dents in front of the pads, but bloody great holes —'

'— which proves,' broke in the commander, 'that it's not only a dog of some kind but a pooch that is more at home sitting in front of someone's fire than out in a field. If it was a foxhound, its claws would be more worn than this.'

'It's a puma. I know it's a puma. The tracks are exactly the same as those by the caravan site,' said the expert.

It was obviously time for some sort of retreat. 'It could be a cheetah,' I said diplomatically. 'I believe the cheetah is the one member of the cat family that does not retract its claws.'

'Don't be silly,' said the expert. 'Everyone knows that the Welsh puma is black.'

That was a bit cheeky of her, I thought, since all I was trying to do was give her a face-saving excuse for one part of her aberration. However, I persevered.

'Well, they may be yellow and spotty in Africa where it's hot and dry, but it wouldn't take them long to be covered in mud if they were over here and that would make them look black.'

Bill was all for covering up as well. 'It could be a wolf, couldn't it, Jimmy?'

'Well, I suppose it just could be a wolf,' said Jimmy thoughtfully.

'If it's not a puma or a cheetah, it must be a wolf,' said the expert. 'But I'm pretty certain it's a puma.'

'But,' continued Jimmy inexorably, 'if you come across a footprint of a fox or a bloody dog in the English countryside, you have to be a bit soft in the head to decide it's a cheetah or a wolf.'

There was really no answer to that one, so Bill spilled his pint all over the bar to create a diversion while the commander hurriedly changed the conversation to the price of sugar beet nuts.

Arthur did his best to kill the story after a couple of weeks, but he was no longer in control. His cracking-point came when the BBC contacted him from London, wanting to send down a camera team to make a programme about the puma. To Bill's disgust, he beat a retreat. He said that he now thought the tracks could have been those of a dog and the vicar had been drunk and might have made a mistake.

The story thrashed around for a few more weeks but, without Arthur's assiduous attention to the various puma nutters who turned up, it gradually began to die away. It never disappeared completely, however. A year after the animal's 'discovery', Arthur found half a dozen Japanese with film cameras working on the story amid the caravans and he still receives a drizzle of enquiries from Americans working on their PhDs. Our puma was even brought in as provenance for the more famous Beast of Exmoor. According to many experts, it was the re-appearance of Arthur's puma, having spent the intervening year or two in travelling there from the caravan site.

Moorview Caravan Site grew rich on the puma. Frank even opened a camp site to sweep up Arthur's leavings but, when he came to the pub to report mysterious lights in the sky, nobody wanted to know.

Chapter Four

NOT MANY tourists made their mark upon our community. Mandy and Keith were one of the few pairs who came down to visit and stayed. They originated from the London area where Keith had been a butcher, owning a couple of amusement arcades on the side, stuffed full of space-invader machines and punk rockers.

Mandy and Keith were an odd pair. It was difficult to think of them as individuals rather than as a couple because they were always together and seemed to view the rest of the world as being populated by couples like them. Their talk was never of the doings of Ivor or of Beryl, but of Ivorandjane and Mickandberyl. In their pair-filled world, the male was always named first, but the village thought of them as Mandyand-keith. They seemed to be a thoroughly innocuous couple apart from their distressing habit of being too nice. They both went around with ingratiating grins on their faces and hers would only fade when she looked at him. He appeared to irritate her when his manner became too close to that of a cocker spaniel, but since hers was very close to that of a springer spaniel, it was felt that she had little to complain about.

They were both in their late forties with black hair. Mandy's must have come from a bottle, but Keith also had a little black moustache which was raven enough to give legitimacy to his hair colour. They bought a tumbledown house, part of a small row of thatched cottages down by the river, and began to do it up.

Mandy was musical, so she told us. Certainly we were all most impressed by the splendid melodies from Rachmaninov to ragtime which wafted through the window of her sitting room. Then Kelvin, the arrogant agricultural patriarch of the pub, passed by one day and spied her seated at the console of some marvellous electronic device. She had her tongue between her teeth in concentration as she laboriously picked out the tune of Beethoven's *Choral Symphony* with one finger, while the silicon chips played the violins and woodwind and harmonized with all the sorts of twiddly bits that suited them.

Mandyandkeith set out to transform their cottage into the ideal 'bijou residence'. Keith's first move was to rip off all the thatch. It was clearly necessary as the straw was rotten and was riddled with rat holes and birds' nests. This action created something of a stir because the local thatcher let it be known that he had not been booked to replace it. His waiting list was nine months long and his charges were quite extortionate, but this was not sufficient excuse to take business away from the community and place it in the hands of strangers. As a result, Mandyandkeith were closely questioned when they next came into the pub. Bill took on this important duty.

'Evening Mandyandkeith,' he said as they came to the bar. Keith ordered a rum and blackcurrant while Mandy asked for a vodka and peach juice. The current landlord found them a bit of a nuisance as he had to stock a variety of soft drinks of cloying sweetness which nobody but them ever ordered. They somewhat made up for this by pumping money into the juke-box in the next-door bar. Mandy liked Barry Manilow while Keith preferred Jim Reeves. They also borrowed all the romantic novels from the mobile library van, to the annoyance of Beryl who had previously had a monopoly on them.

'What are you doing to your cottage, then?' asked Bill bluntly.

'We're doing it up,' replied Mandyandkeith proudly.

'Who's doing the thatch?'

'Keith is,' answered his wife. The rest of the pub stopped playing darts, discussing the weather and trying to look down the front of the landlady's dress and stared at Mandyandkeith with delight and incredulity.

'Is Keith a thatcher, then?' asked Bill.

'Oh no. But it seems to be ever so easy,' replied Mandy. There was a sharp intake of breath round the bar. The villagers had heard the thatcher pontificating about the skills of his trade often enough to know something perilously close to heresy when they heard it. The thatcher specialized in the strong silent look, keeping himself to himself with the dignity of those professionals like brain surgeons, bomb-disposal experts and thatchers. He came from four generations who had crawled about on the roofs of the locality, and we were not used to hearing his trade being discussed with such flippancy.

'Are you going to use straw or reed?' asked Bill.

Keith looked at Bill uncomprehendingly. 'What for?'

'For your thatch, of course.'

Mandyandkeith laughed merrily. 'Goodness gracious!' said Mandy. 'We're not going to use anything like that. It's old-fashioned. Keith's going to use plastic thatch.'

Nobody had ever heard of plastic thatch and so most people found an excuse to walk past the cottage while it was being prepared for re-roofing. Keith ripped out all the old timbers and put in their place an ordinary set of rafters, although they had very little slope to them. This caused a bit of interest as thatch, even plastic thatch, has to have a steep slope, otherwise the water will just seep through the fibres.

Emily Jarrett, one of their neighbours, came into the pub while the roof was waiting for the plastic straw to be delivered. 'It's on,' she announced.

Bill swivelled on his stool and looked at her. She was an attractive woman, but Bill had more respect for the looks of heifers and ewes than for the female of his own species. 'What's on?'

'Mandyandkeith's roof.'

'Don't talk daft. I passed the cottage yesterday and the thatch hadn't even been delivered yet.'

'It came on the back of a lorry this morning and Keith had it tacked into place by mid-afternoon. It came in sheets.'

Everyone, including the landlord, emptied out of the pub and walked down the village to take a look. It was a remarkable sight, a curious yellowy-brown material which bore no resemblance to natural thatch at any stage of its weathering. It was not thick enough, either. A thatched roof billows. It is ample and luxurious, like a good feather duvet.

This looked skimpy, no more than 6 inches deep at the eaves, and one could see the seams between the slabs of moulded plastic.

The onlookers were dumbstruck. The slope on it made it look grotesque. Any raindrop falling on a natural thatch roof can expect an exhilarating ride down a reedy Cresta Run before hurtling off the edge to the ground. On this roof, a raindrop would have been faced with a few moments of grave uncertainty before it managed to work out in which direction it was supposed to travel. The village now contained an aesthetic disaster.

The thatcher went round the village saying 'I told you so' to anyone who would listen and there was some talk of getting the planning authorities involved to tell them to rip off their roof and start again, but an inbred distaste for bureaucrats prevented this from happening.

Mandyandkeith could not see what the fuss was about. Their roof was beautiful, even if it did have the disadvantage of crackling like machine-gun fire as it writhed whenever the sun hit it and forced it to expand. Dennis swore he saw it bring down a low-flying pigeon with a 6-inch nail that shot out of it just as the sun popped out from behind a cloud.

With their roof on, Mandyandkeith continued to beautify the exterior. They painted it baby-bum pink and put in window boxes crammed with poster-painted flowers which, having eerily lasted through the season, were found to be made from plastic. They paved over most of the tiny bit of ground in front of the cottage and filled it with white garden furniture and sun umbrellas surrounding a small fish pond which, Keith told the pub, was filled with shubunkin. Nobody was much the wiser but the word was researched by Ivor and it turned out to mean a kind of goldfish. They installed a wrought-iron gate with its interior in the shape of a heart with an arrow through it and, as a final touch, they changed the name of the cottage from 3 River Lane to 'Pixie's Bower'.

When it was all finished, they held a house-warming to celebrate. They had intended to hold a barbecue on their patio, but the weather had broken. The first gale of autumn was wuthering down from the moor and would have filled their garden with wind-blown umbrellas and shubunkin to the hazard of their guests. All the local heavies turned out. The party was too good a chance to miss of finding out whether the interior of the cottage could possibly match the glory of the exterior.

A bunch of us had come steaming down from the pub with several pints apiece inside us to dilute the sticky concoctions that would undoubtedly be on offer. Mandy had put the organ on automatic pilot and it was moodily amusing itself with a jam session in the background when she opened the door in response to the first few bars of *Home, Sweet Home* on the bell. Mandy, wearing a diaphonous garment the same colour as the outside of the house and bearing a cigarette in a long holder, asked us to take off our shoes to avoid marking the white shag-pile carpet. There was a small altercation in the doorway.

'I'm not taking off my boots,' said Kelvin.

'Do as you're told,' ordered Bill. 'You're not making mucky footmarks all over Mandyandkeith's nice carpet.'

'I'm not taking my boots off.'

'If you won't, you can't come in,' said Bill.

'In that case, I'm not coming in.'

Bill started to laugh. 'I know what it is. You've got holes in your socks and you're embarrassed.'

Kelvin looked sheepish. 'I haven't.'

'You bloody have.' Bill raised his voice: 'Here, Mandy. Kelvin's embarrassed to take off his boots because he's got holes in his socks.'

'Shut up, Bill,' muttered Kelvin.

Too late. Mandy glided up to him in her housecoat. 'Oh! Poor Kelvin! But there's no need to be shy. It doesn't matter if you've got holes in your socks. Just take them off.' Kelvin mumbled and shuffled his feet on the doorstep.

'Take them off!' was the cry that came from an assortment of throats inside the house while Kelvin shot a murderous glance into the hall. Mandy carefully put down her drink – a blue extravaganza – on the glass-topped telephone table inside the front door and placed her cigarette in a silver ashtray with a blue enamelled St Christopher set in the bottom. She turned her back to us and rummaged around inside her housecoat while we politely watched her reflection in the mirror that faced her and pulled down her tights. She turned and strung them gaily round Kelvin's neck.

'There,' she said. 'Now your hostess is barefoot as well and so you have no excuse.'

Grumbling, Kelvin sat down on the doorstep and slipped off his boots, carefully stuffing his thick blue woolly socks inside them before anyone could judge the extent of their holiness. He then entered the house and stood self-consciously inside the hall. We all looked down at his feet. They were a rather nasty pale grey with great gnarled yellow talons which contrasted ill with Mandy's neat little toes with their pearly nail varnish. Hers made one itch to play 'This little pig went to market' on them, while any self-respecting livestock farmer could have improved the look of Kelvin's with the liberal use of a hoof-knife.

'Well, then,' said Mandy brightly. 'Shall we go through to the lounge?' We went through to the lounge. It was already half-full with villagers and I was impressed to see that Barbara, the formidable relict of a colonial judge, had been persuaded to take her shoes off like everyone else and had one foot resting on an embroidered stool.

'The trouble with this village is that too many people talk about damn all,' she was saying, but she broke off and looked round ill-naturedly as the pub contingent came into the room. 'Good God! Now I know what they mean by a bum's rush.'

The lounge was well worth a visit. The ceiling was covered in polystyrene tiles, criss-crossed with beams which half a dozen sets of knuckles immediately investigated to discover that, in spite of worm holes, were plastic. Round the wall hung groups of flint-lock pistols. More surreptitious fondling revealed that these were constructed of the same material as the beams and a surprised buzz ran round the room.

There were four pictures on the wall. All were familiar: a posse of white horses were galloping out of a stormy sea; a blue oriental lady looked down from over the fireplace; Ophelia floated down a river on her back making a daisy chain, and there was a large coloured photograph of the Queen which would have looked more at home in the British consul's office in Benidorm.

Everything seemed to be brand new. There was no evidence of a previous life, no books, no photographs and just a rather pasty-faced teenager to prove that the marrige was of reasonable antiquity. The youth, introduced as Horatio, was helping Keith to ladle out the punch. Dennis graciously accepted a glass, took a sip, looked round for a vase in which to empty his glass and, thwarted, asked Horatio to be directed towards the loo. He came back a minute or so later, looking rather pleased with himself.

'Why are you looking so smug?' asked Bill, who was amusing himself by teasing the organ.

'The loo is just like the rest of this place. Shaggy carpet, fluffy jacket on the bog seat and a poem on the wall: "Please remember, don't forget. Never leave the bathroom wet." I've never seen anything like it.'

'Why should that make you happy?'

'I missed the lavatory and peed on the carpet.'

'That's disgusting,' said Bill.

'Disgusting, but enormously satisfying. I now feel really at home here. I can quite understand why a dog feels the need to cock its leg against the sofa when it enters a strange house.'

'What are you talking about?' It was Barbara who had come over to join us.

'Peeing on the carpet. I've just been to the loo,' replied Dennis, helpfully filling her in on the totality of the conversation.

'A particularly masculine topic. There is nothing more casually destructive to domestic hygiene than the uncircumsized drunken male. You are an appalling sex.'

Mandy came drifting up in a haze of black sobranie tobacco smoke. 'Did I hear someone talking about sex?' she asked archly.

'A greatly overrated pastime,' said Barbara. She looked down at her glass. 'This drink you're dishing out tastes like melted ice lollipops.'

Mandy took a Mata Hari drag on her cigarette while she tried to decide which part of Barbara's statement to respond to. I caught Dennis looking down at her toes which were peeking out from under the lacy hem of her garment. Her toes were definitely her best feature which was rather worrying since it made one wonder if one might be a foot fetishist.

'I don't think sex can be overrated if you are with the man of your dreams and there are lots of men to dream about round here,' said Mandy, fluttering her eyelashes to an extent that would be excessive for an actress in a silent film. Dennis looked at her in alarm. Peeing on her carpet was as intimate as he was prepared to get.

'Do you have any gin?' asked Barbara.

'Or any whisky?' added Dennis.

'Don't you like our Caribbean cocktail?' asked Mandy.

'No,' said Barbara.

'It's quite delicious, but it's wasted on me,' said Dennis. 'I'm perfectly happy with just whisky.'

'I'll go and see what I can do. I'm drinking Bols. It tastes of peppermint and it's a very pretty blue. Would you like to try some?'

'No, thank you,' said Barbara with a shudder. 'Just gin and a little bit of water.'

Barbara got her gin and Dennis his whisky. The room was nicely filled by this time and the level of Caribbean punch in the bowl was rapidly going down. Mandy brought out pretty little eats on the top of biscuits and sausages on sticks which Horatio handed round.

Kelvin found himself in difficulties. He had appropriated a spot which allowed him to tuck his feet beneath the sofa where they were invisible; this, however, meant that he could not go to the food, but had to wait for the food to come to him. He was talking to Mary Mowbray and her laugh, a delightful noise that sounded like a dirty old octogenarian crooning over a pornographic magazine of unspeakable filthiness, was bubbling through the conversation.

Once the food had gone, people began to go round the room making I-am-about-to-leave noises in order to go home to milk their cows and do the chores before the pub opened in the evening. Mandy stood at the bottom of the stairs to supervise the scrum as her guests scrabbled about on the floor trying to locate their footwear.

Kelvin was able to shoe himself first as his high ankle boots with their garland of woolly socks stood out from the ruck of more fashionable footgear. He opened the front door and began to retreat down the path uttering inarticulate cries of gratitude for the hospitality that had been afforded him.

Kelvin's day began to degenerate about then. It was blowing a brisk breeze outside which was ruffling his lank, grey locks. It was also ruffling the roof. Out of the sky, not unlike a particularly low-flying Vulcan bomber, swooped a 32-foot square of plastic thatch which scythed over his head and splashed down amid the shubunkin.

Kelvin's nervous system was never the most reliable of mechanisms, and this encounter with what would have been a

unique demise overloaded its circuits. He sat down on the path. There was a crackling sound from on high and another great bat skimmed over his head and bounced off the fence. He uttered a squawk of dismay and scuttled back up the path on his bottom like a large crab.

'What's going on?' asked Mandy, who was well inside the hall.

'I'm afraid it looks as though the roof of your house may be blowing off,' replied Dennis.

'Don't be silly,' said Mandy.

There was a flapping sound which seemed to come from the upstairs landing and a couple more sheets of thatch thudded down on to the patio outside.

'See?' said Dennis.

Mandy looked and she saw. Holding her cigarette tightly in one hand and her glass in the other, she opened her mouth and emitted one word.

'Keith!'

It was like standing over the vent of a volcano when it exploded. The sheer volume of sound and the quantity of venom contained in that one syllable made people clutch on to doorframes and the wall to prevent themselves being blasted out into the garden where they would have been picked off by the remaining sheets of thatch.

Keith must have known what was liable to be his due when Mandy's decibel count went off the scale in such a way. He moved across the sitting room towards the hall looking like a naughty member of the cabinet answering a prime ministerial summons. He crept through the door, his small black moustache quivering like the whiskers on a frightened hamster and grinned nervously.

'Yes, dear?'

The expression on Mandy's face would have made the Gorgon feel faint with envy. 'That fucking roof you put on is blowing all over the fucking garden!'

The rest of us blenched a little. The local dialect contained all sorts of words – zuggers is one example – which could be used to express any degree of emotion that was felt desirable. This meant that the more standard English epithets were rarely heard. Barbara stepped in where no angel would have dared to tread.

'Really! What appalling language!'

Dennis, a considerably better judge of character and situation than Barbara, tried to shush her, but he was too late. Mandy turned her head towards Barbara, her laser eyes scoring across the mirror that hung on the wall.

'Shut up, you drunken old hag.'

Barbara's mouth opened and shut like that of a shubunkin while Kelvin backed warily out into the garden again, willing to risk being decapitated by a gigantic thatched frisbee rather than face the wrath within.

'Let's go outside and take a look at the damage,' said the commander diplomatically, as Mandy drove Keith into the kitchen with a series of vicious prods in the chest from a rigidly extended forefinger. The door slammed shut behind them and the terrifying sound of a closet termagant letting go on all cylinders rapidly emptied the house of all its guests.

Many of them hurried off home, but the hard core of the curious waited in the garden to see what would happen next. At least two of the shubunkin appeared to have come to a sad end under the impact of the descending roof and were floating, bellies up, on the top of the water while the wind, having done its work, had died down leaving one piece of thatch still precariously stretched across the rafters with a corner of the panel still occasionally flapping sullenly in the breeze.

'Do you think that the party's over?' asked Jimmy, who had been downing Caribbean cocktails with lip-smacking delight.

'I expect so,' replied the commander. 'It doesn't seem right to continue to have a party under these circumstances and I expect that Mandyandkeith will be rather busy trying to weatherproof their house before nightfall.'

'I think we ought to help,' said Dennis.

'They've got a tarpaulin down at the fire station which they use to cover roofs after there's been a fire,' said Bill. 'I'm sure we could use it and it would give Mandyandkeith time to decide if they're going to get in a proper thatcher, or what.'

'I think you would be wise to check with Mandy first,' cautioned Dennis. 'She might have other ideas.'

'Me?' said Bill. 'I don't see why I should have to check.'

Almost unconsciously, we had been edging our way down the garden path to get away from the sounds of Keith having his character, morals and manhood torn to tatters in the kitchen.

'It was your idea about the tarpaulin. So it is you that ought to ask them,' said Dennis.

Bill looked apprehensive. 'But I don't think I ought to interrupt.'

There was the sound of thrown crockery coming from inside the kitchen.

'She always seemed such a pleasant woman,' mused the commander. 'Who would have thought she had a temper and tongue like that?'

The kitchen door was suddenly flung open and Mandy paused momentarily in the doorway, glaring down the hall and through the front door at us, before sniffing with contempt and sweeping up the staircase and out of our sight.

At some stage, the organ had changed over to Wagner and its chips were appropriately blasting out *The Ride of the Valkyries*.

After half a minute or so, a white-faced Keith slunk from the kitchen and came out of the house towards us. It was an awkward situation. Nobody quite knew how to react towards him; whether to make some sympathetic remark to show that we appreciated the ferocity of the roasting that he had just undergone, or whether to act as though nothing untoward had taken place. He cringed at us. Dennis patted him consolingly on the shoulder.

'Not to worry, old chap. We'll soon have a roof back on. Bill says that there is a tarpaulin down at the fire station and we can cover your rafters with it in a jiffy.'

There was a crash from above us and a dozen startled faces looked up. It was Mandy who had flung open her bedroom window and was now leaning out of it, her pink robe billowing round her making her look as if she was about to launch herself upon us like a candyfloss Dracula.

'Don't you dare put a filthy tarpaulin over my roof. It has got to be as good as new by tonight. Kelvin!' Kelvin was backing through the front gate. 'Where do you think you're going? You stay right there and help.' She swept the patio with her eyes. One of the shubunkin suddenly came back to life, sounding like a U-boat on the approach of a destroyer commanded by Jack Hawkins. She withdrew from the window and slammed it shut; a couple of plastic petunias fell out of the window box. There was a pause.

'Nobody talks to me like that,' whispered Kelvin.

'I think Mandy just did,' replied Dennis.

'Well, I'm going,' said Kelvin.

'How very brave of you,' murmured Dennis.

Kelvin hesitated. 'Anyone else coming?'

'I think I might as well come with you,' said Barbara. She looked at Dennis. 'Do you think it would be all right?'

'I'm sure it would be O.K. I can't see our hostess expecting you to clamber all over her roof.'

'Er . . .' said Keith. It was the first time he had opened his mouth since he had come out of the house. There was a bit of colour back in his cheeks. 'I think it would be safer if you stayed.'

Barbara looked uneasily at Dennis who risked a quick glance up at the bedroom window. It was reassuringly closed and the curtains had even been drawn across it. 'I think you can go home, Barbara,' he repeated firmly. 'But I'm not sure that Kelvin had better risk it.'

Barbara scuttled off down the path and along River Lane faster than she had ever been known to move before, without hazarding a backward look. The rest of us stared longingly after her.

'Right,' said Dennis, breaking the spell. 'Let's get going or we'll be here all day.'

We sorted ourselves into a work party to replace the thatch as we had been commanded. There were a couple of difficulties; the workers were wearing their party clothes which were not the most appropriate garments for scrambling about on ladders or on roofs. However, it was Mandyand-keith's ladder and Mandyandkeith's roof where dirt was banned. Even the rafters had been planed and varnished. The other problem was that one of the slabs of roof had disappeared. Eleven had blown off in all and we could find only ten of them. Two were in the pond and the others were either scattered around the garden or over the fence with the neighbours.

Rather surprisingly, Dennis turned out to be the natural leader during this time of crisis and he dispatched the halter, the lamer, the blinder and the older members of the team on a quest to find the missing panel. He was a bit like the captain of a sinking ship sending the weaker passengers to safety before the others.

Keith put up his ladder, which had to cross the window of the bedroom where Mandy was closeted, and Dennis instructed the commander to scale it, reasoning that he must have clambered up plenty of mainmasts and futtock shrouds during his formative years and so would be used to heights. We stuffed hammers, nails and bits of string into his pockets and pushed him, protesting, up the ladder.

He'd got about half-way up, gallantly overcoming the

deleterious effects of the Caribbean cocktails, when the curtain on the bedroom window was whisked aside and Mandy glared out at him from behind the glass. The commander let out a hoarse croak of terror and let go the ladder with both hands. Those on the ground held their breath as he stood on the rungs windmilling his arms and fighting to retain his balance. After a few seconds, he managed to slump forwards and wrap his flailing upper limbs round the uprights.

Mandy must have had experience of the sort of effect that she could have on the weaker sex when she was in the mood because, as the commander watched through the widow like a rabbit paralysed before a stoat, she left the bedroom, shaking the house and making his ladder sway as she slammed the door. We heard her descend the stairs to the kitchen where the odd crashing sound established that she was safely occupied in washing up the party glasses.

It was not difficult to put the thatch back on. The sheets slotted together like Lego and the only complication lay in the fact that Keith had nailed them on and the wind had ripped the plastic off, leaving the nails still embedded in the rafters. Once the commander had hammered them flat, Dennis produced an electric soldering iron and, with the help of a long extension lead, the commander melted dozens of holes in the thatch through which we threaded yards of baler twine, creating a cat's cradle of support that bound the roof to its rafters. The search-and-rescue team found the last panel in the river 200 yards downstream, lodged against a rock, and the commander tied it into place just before the last of the daylight faded.

The roof held safely through the gales of the following winter. It was not quite as pretty as it had been, for the twine made it look as if it had undergone a serious operation and was waiting for the stitches to be removed. It was also rather noisy. Given a stiff breeze, it sounded like a man o' war beating across the Bay of Biscay against a nor'westerly gale and the creak and heave of the straining slabs intermingled with the crash as they fell back against the rafters could be heard over most of the village.

Mandyandkeith settled into the community. Keith found a job in the nearest town as a Kosher butcher with a firm that exported correctly slaughtered and chopped-up bits of animal to London. Mandy sloughed off the air that gave the impression she was always trying to screw up her courage to invite you to a Tupperware party and went around in her true colours as a woman of great power and determination. She even stood for the parish council and achieved the rare distinction of winning only eight votes. Kelvin was distraught. Given that she voted for herself, it still left seven other people in the village who had put their cross next to her name. As Kelvin said, there were seven people who were either mad or bad and he did not know who they were.

Chapter Five

EVERY COMMUNITY has its Shangri-la. For some, it will be the bright lights of London or Borchester. Conversely, the Londoners and Borchesterians will look to Ambridge and the cottage-infested English countryside as the places where the Arcadian myths become reality. As long as the townsmen and the countrymen have the sense to stay at home and dream, all is well. The country cottage is one of the goals for which it is better to strive than to obtain, as the reality can never match the dream. The drains, the water supply and the services are unreliable, while the banks of wild flowers hide piles of garbage because the refuse collector does not call and the centuries of rubbish have to be put somewhere.

Country people no longer spend their idle hours skipping round the may-pole or morris dancing, but watch *Coronation Street* or amuse themselves by observing newcomers with beady, implacable eyes, waiting for the tell-tale signs that show their alienness and their incapacity to handle the simple, everyday problems of the countryside, like overflowing cess-pits and the moles that rampage through their carefully tended lawns.

For our village, the yellow-brick road ended in Canada. Nobody quite knew why this should be but, for generations, those second sons who did not stand to inherit the ancestral acres, and those with some wild oats to sow, went out to the Canadian mid-west for a year or two or for a lifetime.

One of those with a relative somewhere near the Rockies was Jimmy. He was the village's oldest inhabitant who had been a rabbit catcher, retiring with the arrival of myxomatosis. His trade was as irrevocably part of the past as that of a cartwright or a fletcher. Gone are the days when a shotgun fired in the evening at the edge of virtually any field in the parish would have resulted in the death of half a dozen rabbits. The market he supplied has vanished as well, since the housewife no longer buys rabbit to feed her family, the beast having been elbowed out of her cooking pot by the ubiquitous chicken. Gone, too, has the distribution system. The weekly rabbit train, with its wagons groaning under the weight of thousands of furry little carcasses, no longer chuffs along the rural branch lines towards Smithfield. The very lines themselves have disappeared and their routes, marked by neat signposts, are tramped by earnest ramblers from the cities, exclaiming with delight over each weed that infests the decaying foundations of their tracks.

Jimmy was marooned in the last quarter of the twentieth century, a rather small and bow-legged human dinosaur, while the environment which had supported him had vanished forever and even its memory was beginning to fade from people's minds.

Jimmy's life now centred on the pub where he sat for hour after hour over a pint of beer or cider with a baffled look in his eye. The changes that he had seen did not excite or disturb him. He just never understood them or was able to adapt to them. They had just happened. Jimmy never talked much, except when the subject of dogs or cricket came up. Then he would become animated and talk at great length in an accent which Kelvin, no master of the Queen's English himself, described as being as thick as his head.

Jimmy was always listened to, not because his conversation was particularly interesting, but because the hand-rolled cigarette that was always in his mouth stuck to his lower lip as he talked, spraying ash in all directions. Nobody could work out how the cigarette stayed in position and it was a matter of great fascination.

Like many of the old men of the community, he was a widower, living in a cottage in the middle of the village by himself with the granddaughter of his last great rabbiting lurcher for company. In the ancient patriarchal society of the countryside, women have either to dominate their men and make them quake at their every utterance, or risk becoming little better than slaves and be driven to an early grave. Jimmy's wife had died a decade earlier and her epitaph was that she had been 'a good worker'.

A couple of times a year, Jimmy toiled his way past the pub to the churchyard, bearing a bunch of flowers from his garden. These he would place, scattering cigarette ash the while, on the hump under which lay his departed spouse. He would stand there for a few contemplative minutes over her grave and the space beside it reserved for himself before hawking up a gobbet of phlegm which he would send shooting skilfully past his cigarette to the ground.

The tangible product of Jimmy's marriage was a son in Calgary, improbably employed as the financial director of an oil company, who sent his father a Christmas card every year which was shown round the pub. The front always bore a picture of the family. There would be Jimmy's son, looking fat, soft, smug and forty-five in the company of a pretty blonde wife and three fair-haired discontented-looking teenage children. They were always standing in front of a house that looked as if it had been part of the set for *Gone with the Wind*.

Jimmy never expressed any pride in this incongruous outcome of what must have been a very primitive rural coupling, and the rest of the villagers were equally unsure of

the correct response. This family seemed to have so little in common with Jimmy that we would look at the picture, clear our throats uneasily and hand it back to the unemotional grandparent.

One Christmas, the card contained more than the usual 'To the best grandpop in all the world'. There was a PS at the end in a female hand: 'Why don't you come out and spend the summer with us?' The card did its usual round of the pub and we all gazed at the picture, opening it up to study the legend inside before passing it on to our neighbours. It was returned to Jimmy before Winnie asked the question.

'Well, Jimmy?'

'Well, what?' waggled back Jimmy's cigarette.

'Are you going to spend the summer with your family?'

Jimmy screwed up his eyes as a wreath of smoke climbed up over his nose. 'No,' he replied.

'Oh! What a shame. It would be a wonderful chance to see your grandchildren. After all, you may not have many chances left.'

Jimmy looked at her blankly. It had obviously not occurred to him that he might go, any more than he might expect to be asked to lunch by the Queen or go to the moon. Such matters were not part of his life. Others present in the pub also considered Winnie's suggestion. Against it was the fact that Winnie had come up with it. She was fey, arty, wrote doggerel poetry about skipping lambkins and puppies and was a medium who believed that she had a direct line to King Arthur, but, on the other hand, there was no good reason that came to mind why he should not go to Canada. The commander swivelled on his bar-stool and looked over at Jimmy.

'I think it's a damn good idea.'

'I agree,' said Kelvin.

'That's it then, Jimmy,' said the commander. 'The oracle has spoken. If Kelvin says you should go, then you have no choice.'

Jimmy was having none of it. 'Sod off. What would I be doing going to Canada? In summer, too. Who would look after my garden? And who would look after Flossie?'

'I would love to have Flossie to stay,' said Winnie. 'I'd take her for a good long walk every day and the commander would look after your garden, wouldn't you, commander?'

'Get stuffed,' said Jimmy. 'He'd make a mess of everything.'

The commander augmented his pension by market gardening and there was deadly rivalry between him and Jimmy for the Onion Shield at the Horticultural Show every year. The commander may have come to the village wise in the ways of the sea, but his knowledge of the soil was so scanty that he had dug up the best asparagus bed in the county because he wished to clear those odd-looking ferns so that he could grow asparagus. He had eradicated his ignorance through vigorous application, but this was not enough to win the respect of Jimmy who gardened with the instinct inherited from countless generations of peasant ancestors.

'I'll tell you one thing, Jimmy. If you're away over the summer, you'll keep a bit of your pride because you've no hope of winning anything this year. I was talking to one of those northerners who feeds his vegetables on bat's blood and newt's eyeballs. He gave me some tips and my onions'll be like footballs this year.'

Jimmy's cigarette described a derisive parabola in the air. 'I could grow a bigger onion than you if I planted one of those things in the pickle jar behind the bar. Anyway, it makes no difference because I'm not going.'

The door of the pub was flung open and Lindy came bustling in from her rounds. She built up quite a thirst during her district nursing and usually came in to quench it while her husband put their children to bed. 'Not going where?' she asked.

'To Canada,' replied Winnie. 'Jimmy's son has asked him over for the summer.'

'What an excellent idea!'

'I'm not going,' said Jimmy.

'Of course you're going. If you think I'm going to spend another summer cutting your bloody toenails, you can think again. Let some poor Canadian hack away at them for a change.'

'I'm not going,' said Jimmy firmly.

He did not have a chance. Jimmy was no great hand at penmanship and so Winnie wrote off the letter of acceptance to his family and received an effusive reply which made the machinery grind into action. It appeared that Jimmy needed a visa because there was some talk of him having to emigrate due to the intended length of his stay and visas were presented at the regional emigration centre. Jimmy was given a lift up to town by the squire's wife who combined it with a day's shopping. We were told all about the trip that evening. Jimmy was beginning to adjust to the idea of his journey and was quite full of himself.

'I had to answer all sorts of questions and the fellow filled in a great form, all about who I was and even about who my mother and father were. I said you could never be too sure about who your father was and we had a good laugh. He was a Canadian, you know. You could tell by his American accent.'

'Are you all right to go then, Jimmy?' someone asked.

'I reckon so. It all depends on the result of my medical examination.'

There was a rather gloomy silence. Jimmy was thought to be in his late seventies; he smoked thirty lethal roll-ups a day and had done for over sixty years and he sounded as though he suffered from tuberculosis, asthma and farmer's lung all at the same time. He could kill a bluebottle at thirty paces with one of the cannonball gobs of phlegm that he scattered as he went and this, combined with a leg that had been crushed by a carthorse in his childhood, made him look and sound about as healthy as an Egyptian mummy.

'They gave you a medical, then?' asked the commander.

'Yes, it was a rum business.'

'A bit of a cheek, if you ask me,' said Lindy. 'They could have asked your own doctor to do it. What happened?'

'Well, the doctor asked me to cough and, of course, once I'd started, I couldn't stop and that seemed to upset the fellow a bit. Then he stood me up and listened to my chest and then he told me to look at the wall and drop my pants.'

There was a gasp of horror at the idea. Having to examine Jimmy's skinny torso was bad enough, but it paled into insignificance before the prospect of having to root around

among the layers of tweed and grimy long-johns that clothed his nether regions with only the manifest existence of his son to demonstrate that the brave Canadian was boldly going where any human being had gone before. The commander asked the distasteful question.

'And did you drop them?'

Jimmy was unused to being the centre of attention and took a long sip of his cider to fortify himself before answering.

'Well, there was a bit of a problem. You see I didn't quite know what he meant. He was a Yank and so I didn't know whether he wanted me to take down my trousers or my pants. On TV when an American says pants, he doesn't mean pants. He means trousers.'

'So what did you do?'

'I took them all down.' There was a collective shudder. 'Mind you, I didn't like it much. He told me to look at the wall when I was doing it and I didn't like the sound of that. I was a bit frightened that he might make a dive at me. You hear so much about these happies, nowadays.'

'Gays, Jimmy. But I shouldn't have thought that your virtue was in much danger,' said Lindy. 'Did he seem to like what he saw?'

'He didn't exactly say that he liked it. But he did say that he was satisfied.'

'Have you got your visa, then?'

'They said they'd let me know in a week or two.'

The atmosphere in the pub the week or two later could only be described as agitated. Jimmy was gesticulating in the corner while the commander and Kelvin were trying to calm him down with Winnie flapping her arms ineffectually in the background.

'I'm not bloody doing it,' Jimmy bellowed. 'They can take their sodding visa and stick it up their arses.'

'What's up?' I asked Winie. I would have asked Ivor, but he was having a fit of the giggles into his beer.

'Jimmy's been sent a letter by the Canadian doctor. He wants Jimmy to send him a stool sample for analysis.'

'A stool sample!'

'Yes. He's afraid that Jimmy might be harbouring parasites which he would bring into Canada.' She looked across at the indignant Jimmy who had dribbled some cider down his three-day growth of beard. 'I can't say I altogether blame him for wanting to make sure.'

'It's a bloody insult,' said Jimmy.

'Come on,' said the commander. 'It's a very little thing to ask in exchange for a lovely holiday in the Rocky Mountains. Especially when you don't have to pay a bean.'

'It's all very well for you to talk like that, but have you thought about it? Just how do you go about getting a stool sample?'

'Oh, I would think it would be quite easy.'

'Easy? I suppose it would be easy right enough, but so is throwing my cider in your great stupid face. Just because it's easy doesn't mean I want to do it. And sending it to that bloody doctor. What am I supposed to do? Put it in a sodding envelope?'

'A plastic bag might be more appropriate,' said Ivor, controlling his mirth with some difficulty. 'Let's have a look at the letter.' The offending document was passed over for his inspection. 'Hm. It does seem very clear. You have to send a stool for analysis. Right. Have you thought about how you go about it?'

'No,' said Jimmy huffily.

'Well, think about it, man. Don't be so useless. The obvious thing to do is to fish out the sample with a spoon.' We looked at him with distaste. It was Ivor's turn to look huffy. 'What are you all looking at me for? If Jimmy's got to produce a sample, there's no other way of going about it. I would suggest he uses one of those spoons with holes that you use to fish out vegetables and boiled eggs.' There was a heavy silence.

'I ain't got one of those spoons,' said Jimmy eventually. 'Ivor, you must have one. Could you lend it to me?'

'Er . . . well, I'd love to but it belongs to my wife and she's away at the moment and it would be more than my life was worth to lend out any of her stuff.' The commander chortled his disbelief. 'But,' continued Ivor, 'I'm sure that the commander would be delighted to oblige.'

The commander stopped chuckling and looked thoughtful. Jimmy continued to mull over the problem. 'Right, assuming we get as far as using the spoon —'

'I'd cut out the "we", if you don't mind,' said Ivor with a shudder.

'All right. That's fair enough. Assuming that I get hold of a sample. How much do you think that Canadian doctor will want? How big a sample?'

Without Lindy being present to advise, we were all breaking new ground and nobody quite knew. Kelvin was the person who felt he might have something useful to contribute.

'I had the vet round the other day and he took dung samples from the cows to check for worms. He didn't use a spoon but a polythene glove and he just turned it inside out when he'd got a handful and tied a knot in the top to stop any of the shit from leaking out. It seemed quite a good way of doing it.'

'Have you got any of those gloves?' asked Jimmy.

'No.'

'Well, that's a fat lot of good then. We're back with the commander's spoon.'

'You won't need a very big sample if the amount that the vet took is anything to go by,' said Kelvin.

'All right. So I get a little bit. What do I put it in?'

There was a pause while everyone tried to figure that one out. Ivor spoke first. 'Isn't there some sort of law against sending perishable or noxious substances through Her Majesty's mail?'

'I don't see how there can be. Hospitals must be doing it the whole time and Frank Mattock keeps receiving parcels of boar semen which he stuffs into his sows and I wouldn't think you'd be able to get much more perishable or noxious than that,' said the commander. 'I think Jimmy had better use a plastic bag.'

Ivor looked dubious. 'It would be a bit fragile. And if there was a hole in it, as there often is in a plastic bag, it wouldn't be very funny. Although I suppose we could put the bag in a tin to protect it.'

'I know!' said Winnie. 'I've got a little transparent plastic tub of cheese. It's one of those smelly French cheeses but you can't smell a thing. It would be just the job.'

'Have you got an empty pot?' asked Ivor.

'No, but I'd be quite happy to sell Jimmy the one I've got.'

'But I don't like smelly cheese,' said Jimmy.

'You can always give it to someone else,' said Winnie.

'I'll take it off your hands, if you like,' said the publican. 'I always think it's quite nice if there are crisps, olives and cheesy bits around at lunch time on Sunday. It makes the pub a bit classy. I'll use the cheese and you can come round and pick up the empty pot.'

It could never really have been a classy pub but, come Sunday, there were quite a few people around for the moment when Jimmy sidled in, defiantly meeting the stares of the other customers and picked up his tub, the contents of which were covering the little biscuits which mine host had spread over the bar in his attempt to add sophistication to the spit-and-slurry atmosphere of his establishment.

That evening Jimmy was back in his usual chair by the side of the bar.

'All right, Jimmy?' was the greeting that was thrown at him, followed by a more or less subtle request for information on how the proceedings had gone. But Jimmy held his peace, with the ghost of a Mona Lisa smile hovering enigmatically at the corner of his lips.

It was only a couple of days before Jimmy received a response and the letter ended up pinned to the pub wall where it gently turned yellow over the years:

> Dear Sir,
> Thank you very much for the most interesting parcel that enlivened our postbag this morning. However, our doctor actually meant you to take a sample to your nearest hospital for analysis and send the results to this office. I would be grateful if you would have another shit at it.
> Yours faithfully, etc.

Chapter Six

COUNTRY POLITICS are not quite the same as urban politics. Some people do take them desperately seriously, particularly those from the urban middle classes who retire to the countryside and bring their prejudices and fanaticisms with them. They are always to be found as the treasurers and secretaries of the local Conservative associations since nobody else cares sufficiently to see that these mundane political chores are carried out.

The true-born countryman finds politics of lesser importance. They can be a lot of fun, particularly at election time when candidates have their tyres let down and are booed by rival supporters, but the subject of politics is generally a bit of a bore.

This is not an unreasonable attitude to take under the circumstances. The country person's prime interests in life are sex, which politics influences not at all; sport, where again politics has little to offer; and money. On money, politicians do have a peripheral effect but, in the countryside, the main influence on income is not their decisions, world recession or even the doings of Brussels but the weather – droughts, thunderstorms on the ripening corn, or the rain that keeps the tourists away. Since politics do not matter very much, the subject can afford to be treated rather more lightly than it is in the cities and people try to get some fun out of it.

The Bart understood this perfectly. The village was actually situated on the junction between three constituencies, in all of which the Liberals sometimes came first and in all of which the Socialists invariably lost their deposit. One constituency was currently occupied by a rather eccentric Liberal farmer, another by a ghastly new-style Identikit Tory who had been in public relations, and we had the Bart.

The Bart was one of the very last of the great Tory knights of the shires, although he was actually a baronet. He was magnificent from his bristling white moustache down to his Oxford brogues, handmade by Lobb of St James's. He was not part of the new right-wing radical party or even the old liberal wing of the Tories, but believed in an even older tradition which held that the unemployed were all shirkers; those with dark complexions made very good houseboys but were incapable of governing themselves; and that wogs began on the other side of Hadrian's Wall, although there was quite good shooting and salmon fishing to be had to the north of it. He was a much-loved local figure and it was thought that it was only his personal vote that kept the constituency blue.

The Bart used to organize fine, blood-curdling elections. Mobility was the key factor, with the candidates having to rush along the country lanes from village to village to make speeches in schools and halls to stolid voters who were damned if they would give the speaker any encouragement or indication of how they might vote. The Bart would travel with a loudspeaker strapped to the top of his car, greeting most of those he saw working in the fields by name, together with an enquiry as to the state of health of their relations. If the worker

was a known Liberal, he would be subjected to jocular abuse in the Bart's dreadful attempt at a local accent.

It was a tradition that Dick Hunniford, the local Liberal chairman and sheep farmer, should wait in ambush for the Bart when he came to our village and slide in behind his car in a Land Rover with its own speaker on top. Then the two vehicles would cruise round the parish shouting insults at each other with the Bart kneeling on his seat, glaring at Dick through the back window, and thumping on the upholstery in his excitement.

When the Bart decided to retire, even though his party seemed to be re-embracing the principles in which he believed, there were a series of meetings and elections at Tory Party Constituency HQ to select a new candidate. Nobody from our area bothered to attend, and the new man was wheeled round the voters in order to introduce him. It was rumoured that the Bart did not approve of his successor; at any rate, he seemed to have pressing alternative engagements whenever his replacement was scheduled to speak and they never shared a platform. Our village was not one of the more politically significant communities within the constituency and it was not until a good three months after selection that we were honoured by a visit.

The new candidate's publicity had preceded him. He was in his thirties and was an accountant, specializing in corporate taxation. We tried not to hold this against him and turned up *en masse* on the advertised Friday evening. The meeting was at 8.30 pm – a very dangerous time to hold a political meeting, but we were the second engagement of the evening. The pub had been open for several hours and, on a Friday, those were hours that were not to be wasted. So the atmosphere inside the school hall was not ideal.

The room was crowded, rivalling the attendance at the annual pantomime. The venue had advantages as the main meeting place of the village. It was dirt cheap and it was small, which meant that parishioners could easily build up the Roman amphitheatre atmosphere which made for a good political meeting. It also had its drawbacks. The walls were papered with poster-painted children's drawings which could

be distracting, while the chairs with which it was furnished were designed to accommodate well-built six-year-olds. The sight of ranks of adults seated about a foot off the ground, all solemnly staring at the speaker while resting their chins on their knees, had put more than one passionate advocate off his stroke.

The front two rows were occupied by the squire and the rest of the local gentry – all of them a little unruly and nudging at each other. Most of them were slightly drunk and felt themselves back at the level they had last encountered during their first term at prep school.

When Dick Hunniford and the rest of the Liberal committee entered and took up their positions in a standing line along the back wall, there was a murmur of dismay. They had achieved a distinct tactical advantage as they were able to stare commandingly and intimidatingly over the heads of the rest of the voting fodder towards the speaker's podium. The gentry hissed and catcalled their disapproval and one could see their fingers twitching to be filled with bread rolls with which to pelt their rivals. Most of the solidly sober citizens in the rows behind them tut-tutted at their lack of decorum.

The candidate was late and it was 8.45 before Ivor led him in from the school kitchens to a scattering of applause. The candidate looked dangerously smooth – blue pin-striped three-piece suit, black sleek hair and a romantic hero's smile playing at the edge of his lips. Ivor introduced him. Ivor could have mumbled the appropriate grace at a cannibal feast, should he have wanted to. It was one of his greatest talents, and he never wasted an opportunity to fill half an hour with his oratory. All eyes examined the candidate as Ivor chuntered out his skilful platitudes.

He regretfully brought his introduction to an end and sat down to a huge round of applause. The candidate stood up and naturally acknowledged it as his own, while the gentry in the front rows waved their arms about in the air and yelled, 'Encore!' We all knew that Ivor liked to be loved and appreciated, so the clapping continued while the candidate smiled modestly and fiddled with his watch chain. Ivor wore a smirk of delight and self-satisfaction.

The candidate held up a slim, manicured hand in a request for silence. It was not a particularly wise move, although he could hardly have known it. Half his audience were Liberals who were damned if they would do anything that a Tory asked of them and, although the other half were Conservatives, they were enjoying the sight of Ivor grinning like a watermelon as he soaked in the applause and saw no reason why it should stop.

The din of appreciation grew with wild whoops and shouts of 'Speech!' coming from odd corners of the room. Ivor began to realize that the piss was being taken out of him and the mood of barely suppressed hilarity that had taken over the audience infected him as well. It became a joke from which only the candidate, rather pink with pleasure at all the cheering, was excluded.

Eventually Ivor, seated behind the candidate, raised his arm and managed to restore order – barring a few stifled snorts of laughter – and we settled our attention to the serious business of trying to evaluate the Bart's successor. He smiled at us, his head cocked slightly to one side so that the light shone on his glossy black hair creating a halo effect. It was not a smile that said, 'I am trying to be friendly', but a smile that said, 'Look at me. Am I not wonderful? Don't you wish you could smile as attractively as I can?' We shifted uneasily in our seats, but the candidate continued his smile unrelentingly until he was absolutely sure that we had had a chance to savour its full glory.

'Good evening, ladies and gentlemen,' he eventually began. 'I would like first to thank my very good friend, Ivor here, for asking me to come here tonight and for saying such kind words about me and also to say how long I have been looking forward to visiting you.' Ivor looked a little startled at being described as the candidate's very good friend. Not surprisingly, since I had seen him that afternoon hunting worriedly through his desk amid the cow records trying to find the scrap of paper which had been given to him by the constituency agent on which was inscribed the candidate's name. The rest of us just wondered how long he had been looking forward to visiting us. Six hours? Six weeks? Six months?

'This evening I would like to talk about politics and the countryside and how our great party will transform the rural scene.' One of the absurdities about politicians is that they have a grossly inflated conception of the importance of their ideas and actions on the lives of ordinary people. The candidate was no exception.

'We, as a party, are particularly identified with rural issues. We think they are of prime importance, if not of paramount importance. After all, our cities are situated amid the countryside and so it follows that the country is at the basis of our nation. We talk of England as "our country". We do not talk of it as our city. It is our country and not our cities that we talk of fighting to preserve. Ours is the party that wishes to make our country great again. The voice of the country must be heard again, clearly and resolutely, at the conference tables of the superpowers.'

The voice of the country at a summit meeting was a charming idea. A good, clear 'moo' would probably make as valuable a contribution as anything else. However, the candidate had lost most of his audience when it became apparent that he was not one of those politicians who made jokes, and many of them started to doze.

It did not really matter. The gentry, quietly picking their noses in the front row, would have voted for Caligula's horse, had it been a Tory. In fact, they would probably have preferred a horse to anything else. They knew where they stood with a horse: they are honest, reliable, hard-working and have very little of the vanity that drives so many of those who would wish to become our leaders.

The Liberals were also dozing quietly. Even if the candidate had transformed the contents of his water jug into Chateau Lafite before their very eyes, they would have remained implacably opposed to him. They were waiting patiently for question time when they hoped to embarrass him with some carefully planned queries handed to them by the Liberal constituency agent.

Meanwhile the knitting was out in the body of the hall and Kelvin was discussing his harvest prospects with his neighbour. If the candidate had had the sensitivity to be aware of the world beyond the boundaries of his sleek hide, he might have wondered how he had managed to lose his audience so quickly after the rapturous reception he had been accorded.

As Ivor slipped his penknife from his pocket and began to scrape at the accumulation of cow dung beneath his fingernails, the candidate fixed his eyes on the distant landscape of his political Utopia and marched towards the sound of the trumpets.

'I know the importance of the environmental issue and how hard the farmer has to work in ploughing the soil to pay for tractors and . . . er . . . things. I believe that our party does not give sufficient emphasis to the needs of farmers.' He looked at the audience and gathered that not all before him were farmers. 'We intend to give *all* those who live in our rural communities more jobs, better roads and greater access to the landscape. We will give far greater protection to the environment and —' he hurriedly added as a few pairs of cold farming eyes opened and looked at him, '— we will ensure that any such protection does not interfere with the freedom to produce as much food as possible at a good price, which is the glory of our agricultural industry.'

He rambled on as the audience began to shuffle its feet and some of its members, who had partaken of a pint or two earlier, uncoiled themselves from their seats and tripped over feet on their way back to the pub to empty their bladders and pour in some more beer. Seth Matravers heaved himself off his backside and lumbered down his row. His need for a loo was patently absurd as he had the capacity of an oil tanker and he obviously just fancied some more beer. He stumbled over a knitter who stuck a needle into his behind, causing him to fall over the line of gnomes in front of him. The speaker paused while the kerfuffle was sorted out and Ivor seized his silence to tap the side of his water glass with his penknife.

'I am sure the speaker is about to finish and so if people would contain themselves for a minute or two, we shall have a break before questions,' he said.

'Can't you shut the bugger up now, Ivor?' yelled a Liberal wag from the back. The audience, even the Conservatives, murmured their approval and Ivor whispered a few words into the candidate's ear who nodded vigorously.

'In conclusion . . .' he began, but his words were lost in a rising buzz of conversation, the shifting of feet and the machine-gun-fire cracking of joints as people stretched themselves in their cramped seats. The candidate had enough sense to sit down.

'Any questions?' asked Ivor.

Dick Hunniford jumped straight in: 'How are you going to increase returns to sheep farmers?' It was a question that was thrown at every politician who came within hailing distance of the constituency. Not many could give a coherent answer. The Bart's reply had usually been on the lines of, 'I haven't a clue and it's obviously too high as it is, since you look so disgustingly prosperous, Hunniford.' Most politicians tried to bluster to cover their ignorance. The candidate did rather well.

'I am pleased you raised this important topic. The returns

for sheep should undoubtedly be maximized and I believe that our policy should incorporate a double-rated regime in which the cost factor should be in inverse proportion to the EEC unit of account's standing *vis-à-vis* sterling.'

It shut Dick up. In fact, the answer was eventually handed upstairs to the county headquarters of the National Farmers' Union and it took them a fortnight to deliver their opinion that it was probably gobbledygook, but even they were not entirely sure. Dick looked as if he might want to ask a supplementary question after the pause during which we tried to digest the last answer, but Ivor was too experienced to allow his man to be backed into a corner and he slid smoothly on to a more innocuous questioner.

'Thank you. Mrs Baggins, you were next. Would you give your question, please?'

Mrs Baggins was one of the stalwarts of the Women's Institute. There are WIs and WIs. Some are part of the whiteheat of the feminist revolution and organize provocative discussions on the role of rural women in the twenty-first century. Others, more traditional, deal with the interests of their members in the present day. Others, still, prefer to work in the past as most of their members are approaching senility. Ours was into favourite nursery rhymes and competitions about who can produce the prettiest tea-towel and Mrs Baggins was its leading light.

She liked to give the impression of total serenity of nature – a sort of Mother Theresa of the village – but she rather belied the image by dispensing lethal gossip to anyone who would listen, delivered in a breathy whisper through the saintly smile that always adorned her lips. The candidate matched her, smile for smile, as she rose to her feet.

'Our branch of the Women's Institute favours legislation to outlaw glue sniffing. I would like to know whether we can count on your support in parliament.'

'He's not in parliament yet,' shouted a Liberal, and there were a few titters as we waited for his inevitably boring reply.

The smile suddenly disappeared from the candidate's face. 'Er . . .' he said and looked worriedly down at Ivor.

'Did you understand the question?' asked Ivor helpfully.

'Yes,' said the candidate.

'Well, then,' said Ivor encouragingly.

The candidate took a deep beath. 'I feel that this is a very difficult question to answer.' It seemed simple enough and one or two of his listeners forced their eyes open and tried to take an interest. 'It seems to me to be a question of personal morality rather than a subject for legislation. And consequently I would leave it to each individual to make up his or her mind on the matter.' There was a mutter of conversation round the room. Everyone was awake now. Mrs Baggins rose like an avenging angel.

'Do you mean that you won't support such legislation?'

The candidate looked round nervously. His smile was very fixed. 'I am afraid you are correct. Such a law would be a step back to Victorian times and, although I heartily disapprove of such practices and avoid it myself, I feel that parliament should not become involved. I think it would be electorally disastrous to pass such a law and the law itself would be unenforcable.'

This was baffling stuff indeed. Most unexpectedly, the candidate appeared to have at least one opinion of his own. Even more unexpected was the nature of that one opinion. Mrs Baggins rose to her feet again, her smile of serenity now absent.

'I've voted Tory all my life, but I think your attitude is disgraceful. I don't think you deserve the support of decent people. You seem perfectly content to watch our children corrupted and destroyed.'

There was an outraged rumble of support from the Liberal contingent and even the Tories looked a little shocked. It had been a perfectly mundane question, requiring a perfectly mundane answer, but the candidate had skidded wildly beyond the barriers of mainstream politics and was thrashing his way through a minefield of his own creation. He looked at Ivor for support with a film of sweat on his brow, but Ivor was embarrassedly examining his nails once more. The candidate was on his own.

'I am very sorry that you feel that way but, I repeat, however unpopular it might make me in some reactionary quarters, I feel that the problem is one of personal morality and is not a fit subject for legislation.'

There was a storm of hissing, in the middle of which Dick rose majestically to his feet.

'I am sure I speak for everyone in our community when I say that reactionary is not the word that I would consider applying to this dangerous practice. Any man who is not prepared to do all he can to stamp out glue sniffing does not deserve to get to the House of Commons.'

There was a bay of agreement from the audience, even from the front rows. The candidate looked wildly round him and suddenly began to snort with laughter, doubling up over the desk in front of him. Ivor looked at him in consternation and jumped to his feet, ready to bring the meeting to a close in case the man was about to break down. The candidate waved him down, still laughing. The audience quietened down, wondering what on earth he was about to do or say next.

He took a large silk handkerchief out of his pocket and mopped his eyes. 'I am most frightfully sorry. Of course I support legislation against glue sniffing.' He started to giggle again. 'I thought the questioner said she wanted legislation outlawing loose living.'

That was the making of the candidate. It had looked as if there would be serious defections from the ranks of Tory supporters with the retirement of the Bart, but now we had the Sniffer. In the next twenty-four hours, the tale went round the constituency and his succession to the Bart was secured.

He even managed to increase the Tory majority.

Chapter Seven

LOVE MAY make the rest of the world go round; in our village, however, it wasn't love that did the trick, but gossip – often gossip about love. If the facts were not available, they were invented, and so it was usually in the interests of those who feared they might be gossiped about to make sure that the information in general currency was accurate. If accuracy could be compromising, their story had to be sufficiently convincing or interesting to ensure that their desired version would be accepted rather than the reality.

The pub, of course, was the general clearing house for news and scandal, where anything doing the rounds could be tested and embellished. How queer was the local hotelier? Was his *penchant* for the sort of sweaters that are worn on breakfast television sufficient evidence to confirm his aberration? Was Tony nicking diesel fuel from Ivor? And were the remarkable efforts of the shepherd to guard his privacy proof that he had something to hide? Could he be more attached to his charges than he might care to admit? Such things were not particularly rare in the countryside and he always wore gumboots.

Kelvin was sophisticated enough to know that very little can ever remain a secret in the country and, when he decided to enliven his private life, he instinctively involved everyone else in the affair. Kelvin had been quiet on his domestic front for years, ever since his long-suffering wife had died during a nasty dose of influenza. It had been felt that she had probably seized the opportunity of a peaceful demise and put a half-nelson on the Grim Reaper until he agreed to take her away with him.

Kelvin's life had been a model of decorum since then. His mousy, middle-aged daughter, Prudence, kept house for him and it was presumed that he got his jollies by tyrannizing her, just as he had tyrannized his wife. But Kelvin came into the pub one day bearing a copy of a farming magazine, looking as smug as a Friesian calf who was suckling a Jersey cow.

'Why are you looking so pleased with yourself?' asked the commander. His only concession to his naval past was that he occasionally wore a dark blue blazer with anchors on the brass buttons.

'Have you read *Farmers Weekly*, then?'

'Why? They're not featuring the amazing Kelvin Morchard cattle-rearing system, are they? Stick them in a field for eight years and then sell any that haven't died of old age.'

'I make a better living than you,' replied Kelvin, rather nettled at being summed up so easily and accurately.

'I doubt that. You don't have a munificent index-linked pension as do we who have retired from the sounds of strife.'

'That sound being ice cubes clinking in your pink gins.'

'We can all choose our own careers and you will not have heard me complain. Anyway, why are you looking so uncharacteristically cheerful?'

'I've got an advert in this week.'

'What's it about? Trying to sell your soul? It won't be worth much.'

Kelvin's sense of humour was the least developed of his faculties and so he ignored this crack. 'Read my advert,' he said, brandishing his magazine at the commander. The latter took it, placed it on the bar, put on a pair of gold-rimmed spectacles and read at the indicated place in a loud, clear voice so that the rest of the pub could hear.

'Personable, middle-aged widower with own farm seeks housekeeper/companion. No dogs. Send photograph. Apply Box.' The commander took off his glasses and howled with laughter. Kelvin bristled as the rest of the pub joined in.

'What's the joke?'

The commander wiped his eyes. 'Kelvin, you shocker. It's against the law.'

'What's against the law? You're allowed to advertise for a companion. It's not as if I'm asking for someone to give

French lessons or to administer discipline or do one of those kinky things.'

'No, it's not that. The Trades Description Act. You haven't been middle-aged for twenty years and nobody has considered you personable since the day your mother died.'

'Don't be so bloody rude. I'm still in the prime of my life. I can still put in a day's work that would see off any of the young whipper-snappers about nowadays.'

'Kelvin, my dear. This advert of yours is going to bring down hordes of women, all of whom will be after your money. It'll even bring down men as well, because there's nothing about which sex you require.'

Kelvin snatched the magazine. 'Isn't there?' He read the

advertisement again. 'But it's obvious isn't it? Housekeepers are always ladies, aren't they?'

'I wouldn't count on it. If you can have female prime ministers, you can just as easily have male housekeepers.'

'That sort of fellow won't read *Farmers Weekly*. I'm just after a nice lady who might be able to help a bit with the bullocks and that sort of thing.'

'You might find someone who's good at "that sort of thing",' agreed the commander. 'But I doubt if she'd be much good with the bullocks. And what's Prudence got to say about this? She's been looking after you for ages and she'll be a bit put out if some woman moves in as lady of the manor.'

Kelvin had obviously not given much consideration to Prudence's feelings. She was only a heifer, after all, and it was beginning to look very unlikely that she would be bred from. A few young bulls had sniffed around her when she had reached prime breeding condition fifteen years earlier, but her unfortunate conformation, temperament and her highly suspect pedigree, having a sire like Kelvin, had frightened them all off. This was in spite of the fact that she would be the sole inheritor of the farm when Kelvin went to the Great Pastureland in the Sky.

'Prudence? Oh, she won't complain. She always does what she's told.'

'What do you want someone else for, then?'

'Well,' replied Kelvin coyly, 'you never know what might turn up. I might even want to get married again.'

'Who would want to marry an old goat like you?' said Bill scornfully.

'You'd be surprised,' said the commander. 'Clean him up a bit and he'd be quite a good catch. Single man with a few bob.'

'I ain't got a few bob,' said Kelvin hurriedly. Like all established farmers, he liked to look over his rolling acres and claim that the bailiff was virtually at his door. 'So why don't you buy me a drink?'

Kelvin thrived in a rural habitat among those of his own kind, but he was smart enough to be aware that the wool could be very easily pulled over his eyes by his urban brothers, let alone their sisters. Although there was the obvious danger of exposing himself to ridicule, he knew that he could get himself into terrible trouble if he tried to deal with the replies to his advertisement by himself. Quite apart from anything else, he, like so many of his generation of farmers, was barely literate. So both he and the rest of us thought it would be a good idea to go over the replies to his advertisement together. That way he could at least share the responsibility for any disaster.

We did not see anything of Kelvin for a while, during which time we assumed that all the ardent damsels of the country who fancied the idea of a personable middle-aged widower with a farm were licking the tip of their pencils and rushing out to buy stamps and writing paper. Kelvin came back into the pub a couple of weeks later, bearing a sackful of potatoes.

Being one of the godfathers of the parish through his possession of the only flat field in the area – the sole possible venue for fêtes and gymkhanas, for which his permission was consequently required – he could enjoy certain little perks. His main one was the right to supply the pub with agricultural produce of all kinds.

The pub provided sandwiches and snacks for the benefit of culinarily primitive tourists, which meant that potatoes, milk and eggs were all needed, and the landlord paid cash, or with credit in the bar which was just as good. Every time a new landlord took over after the previous one had declined into helpless alcoholism, all these supplies would be put out for tender, but the other farmers respected the conventions and Kelvin's tender was always unopposed. So Kelvin entering bearing a sack of spuds, dead chickens or milk was a normal event. The fact that his bar chit was usually well in credit, did not make him any more generous when it should have been his round.

'Is that my spuds?' asked the landlord.

Kelvin looked shifty. He often did. In fact he usually wore a shifty expression on his face, or else one of bluff bonhomie which he used to cover the fact that he was feeling guilty.

'Spuds? I haven't got time to do spuds at the moment. Me and Prudence are flat out doing the haymaking. It's the first decent bit of haymaking weather we've had this summer. We've baled 10 acres today and, if the weather holds, we'll do the same tomorrow. Prudence is turning the swaths now.'

Kelvin was one of the very few local farmers who still relied on hay as the mainstay of his winter stock-feeding system. It had dawned on most of the others that the weather was the great unpredictable in their working lives and, in order to make decent hay without resorting to expensive artificial drying, they needed to be able to count on four or five days of settled weather.

It has been proved over countless years of careful observation that Nature waits until haymakers cut their grass, ruffle it, and backcomb it into neat rows, before she releases a barrage of good rollicking thunderstorms. The thunder was grumbling in the distance even as Kelvin ducked in the pub door.

'Did you have any replies to your advert?' asked the commander.

'Which advert?' asked Kelvin.

'The one for housekeeper and things.'

'Oh! That advert. Well, now you mention it, there were one or two. I was hoping you might be able to help me a bit.' Slightly shame-faced, Kelvin lifted the potato sack on to the bar and plunged his hand inside. He brought out a fistful of letters and handed them to the commander.

'Good grief!' exclaimed his companion. Kelvin put his hand inside the sack and brought out more letters, and then more and handed them round.

'This is positively terrifying,' said the commander.

'That it is,' replied Kelvin. 'I've even had women writing to me from abroad.'

'What are you going to do about them all?' asked Lindy, who also constituted part of Kelvin's fascinated audience.

'I thought I might have an open day on the farm and ask them all down.'

'You'd be crazy!' said the commander, to grunts of agreement from everyone else. 'Can you imagine a hundred women, all wanting a personable middle-aged widower, being confronted by an arrogant old lecher like you? Not to mention

Prudence. You'd need police protection and they'd still probably murder you. And they could claim justifiable homicide and no jury would ever convict them.'

'But how else can I ever select from this lot?' said Kelvin despairingly.

'Are you sure you want to get involved with the sort of women who would reply to an advert like this?' asked Lindy.

'Oh yes. There are enough of them here to make sure I can get a woman who will do what I tell her. That's the trouble with the country today. Too many women have got minds of their own. A woman needs a man like me to do her thinking for her.'

'In that case, there would be no thinking at all taking place,' said Lindy sarcastically.

'That's the sort of thing I mean. No woman that I would want would ever talk to me disrespectfully like that.'

As Kelvin did not appear to know how to begin the process of selection, the commander took charge in a manner befitting someone with his experience of administration and man-management. 'First of all, we need to know the parameters of your requirements,' he said, preparing to make a list.

Kelvin looked uncertainly at Lindy who explained for him. 'He means we need to know what you want. Like blonde hair or long legs, for example.'

'Oh yes. Well, I'm not so worried about the legs or the colour of her hair, but I wouldn't mind a big pair of . . . er . . . bosoms.'

The commander looked distastefully at Kelvin. 'That's not quite what I meant, but we'll mark it down. Age?'

'Sixty-three.'

'Not you, you fool. What age do you want your lady to be?'

'Oh, sorry. I hadn't really thought about it.'

'Well, think about it now, man. What's the oldest that you want her to be?'

'Hmm. I certainly wouldn't want her to be too old although, if she was over sixty, she would be collecting a pension. How about fifty-five? That's a good age.'

'Right,' said the commander, marking it down. 'What's your bottom limit?'

'I don't really think that matters, do you?'

'Would you want a seventeen-year-old?'

'That would be a bit young, I think. She ought to have had some experience of life.'

Lindy snorted. 'I should think the average seventeen-year-old these days has had a damn sight more experience of life than you, Kelvin.'

'I don't reckon so. Anyway, I think it's only right that she shouldn't be any younger than Prudence. Prudence might find it difficult to get on with a stepmother who was younger than her, if it comes to that.'

'That's sensible,' said the commander approvingly. 'How old is Prudence?'

'She'll be thirty-eight this Michaelmas.'

'Right. We'll put a bottom limit of forty. Now, height and weight?'

'I don't mind about that.'

'Looks?'

'No, I don't mind. So long as she's not really ugly. I mean, I've got my pride. I wouldn't like people to think I was desperate. And she's got to be, you know, big.' He sketched a curve in the air with his hands.

'You've already said that, Kelvin,' said Lindy.

'But the commander didn't mark it down. I was watching.'

'All right, Kelvin.' The commander scribbled 'Knockers, two, enormous.' 'How's that?'

'That's fine.'

'How about children?'

'Oh, I'm not so sure about that. I'm a bit old to be a father now, and Prudence might get a bit upset if I went and sired any more.'

'No,' said the commander patiently. 'I was not talking about your future plans. Would you mind if she brought any children with her? I would imagine that quite a lot of these women might be divorced or separated and might well have children in their charge.'

'Oh, sorry. I see what you mean.' Kelvin thought for a bit. 'I think it would be best if I said no female children and no boys under twelve.'

'What have boys got that girls haven't?' asked Lindy curiously. 'Apart from the obvious?'

'I could do with a bit of help round the farm and a strapping teenager could be quite useful.'

'Ah! I see. Cheap labour.'

'That's right,' replied Kelvin without a qualm.

'It's going to be a very spiritual relationship,' said the commander. 'However, we're beginning to get some sort of picture. I think we should move on to interests. There may not be any indication in the letters, but are there any hobbies or interests or anything like that which you feel are important?'

Kelvin thought again. You could always tell when Kelvin was thinking deeply because you could see his lips move. When he was reading, he not only moved his lips but whispered aloud. He came to his conclusions: 'Cooking, sewing, cleaning, working on farms, sheep, cattle, hens, calves —'

'Slow down a bit, I'm trying to write all this down.'

Lindy looked at the list with distaste: 'I pity anyone who ends up with you, Kelvin.'

The commander also examined the finished list. 'Right. I suppose we'd better start looking through these letters to see if we can find anyone who remotely matches this paragon.'

There was a general filling of pints as the letters were distributed round to those who could read anything more than the figures on their market cheques. Most of the letters contained photographs and these were passed over to Kelvin for his examination. We took an unspoken mutual decision to ignore any letters whose writers showed that they possessed any degree of refinement or sensitivity. No delicate flower or hothouse plant could be subjected to the crude blasts of Kelvin.

We ended up with three candidates. One was a fifty-year-old who showed all the desirable interests, having been a farmer's housekeeper for years. Against her was her demand for a bedsit of her own with a colour TV with a minimum screen size of 22 inches. It was thought that this showed a hard-headedness which militated against Kelvin consummating his carnal desires with her.

The second letter came from a farmer's widow, age unmentioned, but she had a son of thirty. Her application seemed to be rather ulterior in its motives as she wrote of how her son had been cruelly deprived of the opportunity of taking on her late husband's tenancy. It appeared that there might be a distinct possibility that Kelvin might find himself poisoned once she had managed to change his will in her favour.

The third candidate was the one that was most interesting.

She enclosed a photograph that showed her in a bikini on a Costa Brava holiday. The applicant stated that she was forty-two and the picture must have been taken, according to Lindy, at least a decade earlier since she was sure that the remarkable suspension of her two huge mammary glands would have begun to fail under the forces of gravity by her fourth decade. She was childless, twice divorced, lived in London, was fond of the countryside and 'a good time'.

Kelvin found himself in a bit of a dilemma. He liked the idea of a thirty-year-old, an experienced farm worker, who could be strung along with a series of vague promises about the future and who might even provide a partner for Prudence. But the photograph of the two enormous knockers, even if they had begun to succumb to fair wear and tear, had him dribbling into his beer with excitement. Lust won. He decided to write to her.

'What sort of salary do you intend to offer?' asked Bill.

Kelvin looked at him in alarm.

'Salary? Do you think I will need to pay her? I would have thought that offering her board and lodging would have been enough. You don't pay a wife a salary.'

'You don't pay a wife because all your worldly goods are already endowed to her. Unless you intend to do that on the strength of a magnificent pair of breasts, I'm afraid you will have to pay her. After all, you did advertise in the "Jobs Vacant" column,' said the commander.

'I suppose I'll have to come to some arrangement then,' he said begrudgingly. 'But let's not dwell on the subject of money. What's the next step?'

'How do you mean?'

'Well, do I ask her down for an interview, or should I just hire her?'

'I think the best thing to do would be to write as honest a letter as you can manage so that you don't waste each other's time. She might have her own parameters. For example, middle aged, to her, might mean around thirty-five instead of sixty-three. It would be a shame if you paid her fare down and she got straight back on the train as soon as she clapped eyes on you.'

Kelvin pondered deeply over this. 'Do you think you could help me to write a letter, Commander?'

'With pleasure. I'll draw something up and you can copy it out.' The commander selected an envelope from the pile of letters – a pink one that smelled of Lily of the Valley. 'Dear Madam,' he said as he wrote.

'Don't you think that's just a little formal under the circumstances?' asked Bill.

The commander considered. 'I wouldn't have thought so. Kelvin hasn't met her so she doesn't know his name or anything. I would certainly use "Dear Madam" and sign off with "yours faithfully".'

'It's a bit old-fashioned and even intimidating,' said Lindy. She might disapprove, but she was not going to be left out.

'Good manners are never old-fashioned,' said the commander. 'And Kelvin is supposed to be her prospective employer.'

'From what I can make out, neither she nor Kelvin are aiming for a conventional working relationship. She's more likely to chuck him under the chin and call him "ducks", rather than stand to attention and call him "sir". Don't you agree, Kelvin?'

'I think "madam" is a bit formal. Couldn't I just say "Dear Missus"?'

The commander frowned. 'I suppose you can call someone "missus" in speech, if you must. But you certainly can't when you're writing a letter. I suppose we'd better use names.'

Kelvin picked up her letter and studied it. 'She's called Matilda Billingsley.'

'Right,' said the commander. 'We'll start off: "Dear Mrs Billingsley, Thank you for your letter in reply to my advertisement for a housekeeper/companion. It is only right that I should tell you a bit more about myself. I am sixty-three —" '

'I don't think I ought to say that,' interrupted Kelvin.

'I don't see why not. It's true, isn't it?'

'Yes, but it's a bit blunt. There's sixty-three and sixty-three. Jimmy there has looked at least ninety ever since he has been in his fifties and I wouldn't want her to think I was like that.'

'You don't want to mention your age?'

'I think we ought to mention it, but just lie a bit.'

'How big a bit?'

'Say I am a young fifty-seven.'

'Right: "I am a young fifty-seven and I have been a farmer all my life." How's that?'

'That's fine. I think it would be a good idea if you said I was good-looking or something like that.'

'I don't honestly think you can get away with that,' said Lindy, looking at Kelvin critically. 'Unusual looking, perhaps, but your nose is too big and your false teeth don't fit well enough for you to be described as good-looking.'

'You ain't no oil painting yourself.'

'I agree. But it is not me that is claiming to be one. I think you could fairly call yourself interesting-looking.'

'Thank you,' said Kelvin.

'Because that could have even taken care of Quasimodo.'

'Who's he?'

'A Frenchman who looked not unlike you.'

'I see. OK. I'll agree to that. Say: "I am an interesting-looking young fifty-seven." '

'If that's what you want,' said the commander. 'It's a bit personal, though, isn't it? After all, you're just offering a job.'

'It's a personal sort of a job. What else does she say in her letter?'

Lindy picked it up and skimmed through it. 'She says she is a driver and has a mini. Perhaps we should say that you have a car.'

'I don't think Kelvin's clapped-out van is worth mentioning,' said Bill. Kelvin's clapped-out van was looking even worse than usual. He used it to transport lambs and bales of hay round the farm. Moreover, the previous week, a curious cow had put its head through the window and, when it had tried to pull its head back out, the whole door had come off its hinges and the animal had worn it like a giant collar for several hours before it could be removed.

'I've got a Morris Minor,' said Kelvin.

'But that belongs to Prudence,' said Bill.

'It's in my name. Put down a car, a Land Rover and two tractors. That ought to impress her.'

The letter was duly written and sent off. The village waited for Matilda Billingsley's response with as much patience as it could muster.

Chapter Eight

BILL STARTED up a book, offering odds of 2 to 1, that Matilda Billingsley would not turn up and, if she did, the odds climbed to 20 to 1 against her taking the job. He found few takers.

It took a week for a reply to come back from London where the lady lived. 'Dear Kelvin,' it started off, without any of the formality that we had agonized over, 'I am most interested in this position,' which occasioned much ribald delight. Since she was a 'shy girl at heart', she would much rather meet Kelvin in London for the first time than come down to stay. She found Kelvin a very pretty name and preferred 'mature men rather than young men because they are older'. The gist was that she would meet Kelvin at Paddington and they could spend a week-end together to see how they would get on.

Kelvin was terrified at the prospect. He had once been to Smithfield, but his only other forays out of the parish were his fortnightly trips to the local market where he met his cronies in the pub and they became gently sozzled together. Kelvin was as territorial as a cockerel and his patch was the parish and the thin ribbon of land to the market. He knew almost everybody on his territory and they knew him and he understood all the surprises and emergencies that were likely to arise and how to deal with them.

Away from his own patch, particularly in London, Kelvin knew that he would be nothing but an elderly man with scruffy clothes and a country-bumpkin accent. He would be in no position to impress Matilda Billingsley with his land, his cattle, his friends; that he was the only man in the village who could run a slate at the pub or that he had been on the parish council for thirty years. Not even for the sight of Matilda's chest was he prepared to strip himself of his identity to that extent.

Perhaps Matilda felt the same. At any rate, it took another five weeks of negotiation before she agreed to come down to the countryside to investigate the position that was vacant. Kelvin had even been forced to mention money and had thrashed out a salary of £42.50 a week, plus room and board.

The great day arrived. Kelvin had to go into town to meet the train at about 8.00 pm and he visited the pub to give himself a bit of Dutch courage before he left. He looked ghastly, wearing his wedding/funeral suit with a white carnation in his button-hole to aid recognition. His collar was sawing into his neck and already grey spikes of hair were slowly re-erecting themselves on top of his thoroughly watered scalp. If his false teeth had been up to the challenge, he would have been biting his fingernails. A couple of whiskies were poured down his throat and he departed to meet his destiny.

This was on a Friday evening. The next night was the communards' barbecue. This had become one of the social high spots of the year, along with the Christmas dance in the skittle hall behind the pub and the midsummer Strawberry Ball organized by the hunt.

The barbecue was usually a highly successful affair. The commune lived secretively for most of the year, trying to be self-sufficient, creating dreadful pieces of pottery and paintings, studying strange religions and descending like locusts on the local jumble sales to rummage through the clothes. Three centuries ago, the villagers would probably have raided the commune and burned most of its inhabitants at the stake, but now they were just looked at with amused tolerance and this they repaid at the barbecue. The commune laid on a rodent's feast of nut stews and home-fermented wines while the locals brought along bits of pig and chicken for barbecuing and hip-flasks full of spirits so that the country wines could have a rocket-assisted start in the task of inebriating everyone.

There had actually been a moment earlier in the year when it looked as though the communards might be cast out into social darkness. One of them had given birth to a child, thus settling a local controversy as to her sex, and had thrown a party to celebrate the event. Unlike the barbecue, it was primarily a communard party with alternative livers from all round the county coming together to get pissed, stoned, pass round the infant's horoscope and gibber to the moon. A few locals had attended just to be sociable, and an awful tale had emerged through them.

One of the dishes on offer had been a pâté. Since it was the only meat as opposed to veg dish, the locals had tucked in. The hostess had drifted up to them in her kaftan, offering a puff of her acrid, hand-rolled cigarette.

'Do you like the pâté?'

'Oh yes. It's delicious.'

'I'm so glad. In nature, I noticed that all animals like to eat their own placentas and so I made the pâté out of mine.'

During the ensuing uproar, even the other communards had thought that this was just a little over the top and the lady had been asked to leave. She had moved on to a more sympathetic establishment in Cornwall, but there was still a degree of gastronomic unease about the barbecue, while the grass-and-dandelion salad was even less in demand than usual.

It was known that Kelvin would be bringing his Matilda to the barbecue and so most people turned up promptly at 9.00 pm, rather than drifting in as the pubs closed. The party was held in the courtyard of the old stable block. Given a hundred thousand pounds or so, the communards could have had an establishment fit for a merchant banker wishing to become a country gentleman. Their house was a late Georgian vicarage, but it had been browsed over by pests for decades, housed thriving colonies of fungi and had been empty for five years before the communards had taken it over.

The communards themselves had come down to the neighbourhood with a reputation of being drug-sodden degenerates. For all we knew they probably were, but they seemed quite harmless as they pottered about on their 6 acres of land, trying to grow their food organically and fighting a losing war against the hordes of encroaching nettles and thistles which had not had such an easy life since the invention of herbicides.

The only member of the community who worried much about the habits of the communards was Percy the policeman, and he had been keeping a low profile since his last brush with them. He had espied two of their number walking through the village towards the river and had observed one of the communards pass an object to the other in a furtive and suspicious manner. As he approached them, the communard holding the suspicious substance had stuffed it into his mouth in a clear attempt to get rid of the evidence. Percy had pounced with an outstretched hand and commanded the masticator to spit the evidence into his waiting palm. The obliging fellow duly disgorged a mouthful of well-chewed peanuts, to the delight of the dozen or so watching tourists. Over the ensuing couple of weeks, Percy had been greeted by locals offering to spit in his hand wherever he went and he had become rather browned off by it.

As it happened, the communards had fortuitously entered an area that was probably more tolerant of drugs than most. There was nothing particularly exceptional about the amount of alcohol that was consumed, massive though it was, but the older families in the neighbourhood had always enjoyed their own means of intoxication. On the moors above the village grew quantities of hallucinogenic fungi which were latched on to by the hippies of the sixties as one of the paths to enlightenment. For centuries the locals had harvested them for consumption at autumn social get-togethers and nobody had ever given it a thought. It was really rather embarrassing for so many solid citizens to discover that they were among the pioneers of the drug culture. So we tolerated the strange customs of the communards where other communities may not have done.

The barbecue got under way, running its loud, midgy, smoky course. The fire lay at the centre of the courtyard surrounded by bales of straw on which to sit where one swithered between the twin evils of being eaten alive by insects or swathed in the greasy smoke coming from the broiling pigs and chickens on the grill.

The squire's wife was deep in conversation with Ben Moggridge on the breeding habits of the goat. Ben called himself a tree surgeon, which meant that he spent the summer sawing up logs to stoke all the wood-burning stoves in the locality, owned by those who had not yet worked out that they were both highly expensive to run and very inefficient.

There was still no sign of Kelvin and Matilda, and an air of restless anticipation prevailed. The dancing that was going on in one of the stables had a frantic feel to it and some of the old ladies of the parish were kicking up their heels for the first time in decades to the heavy metal music being pumped out by the commune's ghetto blaster. Assorted dogs scrabbled and snarled like their ancestors at medieval banquets for scraps of meat thrown into the darkness beyond the circle of straw bales. Not just bones were coming their way, but prime New Zealand lamb chops and sausages, sent spinning into the night after one horrified bite through the carbonized exterior had revealed the chill, deep-frozen heart within.

Then things began to happen. Whether Kelvin arrived late so that he could make a grand entrance or so that he could sneak in and lose himself in the milling throng was unclear – although his choosing the modest alternative would have been totally out of character, however exceptional the circumstances.

Kelvin was not wearing his suit and was looking more comfortable in his 'number two' dress of wide-bottom grey trousers and dung-coloured sports jacket. However, the sudden hush that fell over the assembled multitude as the murmur of talk died away and the auditory vacuum was filled by the sound of sizzling fat and the thump of music from the stable was not because we were interested in the fine detail of Kelvin's dress but because we were interested in the lady.

The first noticeable thing about her was that she tottered on heels that appeared dangerously high. High heels are not common in the countryside as they sink in where the tarmac stops and a slip on a cowpat can have dangerous consequences. Her stated age of forty-two seemed to be a fair approximation, but the extent to which the passing of the years had slackened the ligatory guy-ropes that kept her undeniably astounding breasts in their state of suspension was difficult to ascertain

since they seemed to be incarcerated in a curious conical brassiere.

With a hand resting genteelly on Kelvin's arm, she tottered into the light of the fire and there was a mighty hiss of indrawn breath. She was wearing a cotton frock covered in pictures of ponies, a concession no doubt to the countryside, but it was a very thin garment and there was a definite nipple-shaped protuberance to the fore – well to the fore. Either she was not wearing a bra at all, in which case she was a physical phenomenon on a par with Cliff Richard, or she had holes in the front of it which gave rise to all sorts of erotic speculation. She was a powerful-looking woman – not tall, but broad, with her superstructure neatly balanced by an equally formidable backside. Her face, with its surrounding tight blonde curls, was saved from vapid prettiness by a slightly underslung jaw which gave her a faint resemblance to a salmon.

There was something odd about her manner. Apparently not at all shy about being thrown among strangers in rather unusual circumstances, she seemed totally unaware of being scrutinized by a score of pairs of eyes. She stared intently at the barbecuing meat and, after a decent interval of contemplation, switched her attention to the bar with its barrel of cider and boxes of British wine spread amongst the odd-shaped assortment of bottles of home-brewed beer and wine.

With Kelvin standing by her side like an abashed schoolboy, she then switched again, letting her eyes travel round the courtyard, taking in the straw bales, the people sitting on them and the stable doors through which the music was coming. She then finished up by staring back at the fire and following the plume of smoke upwards to the moonlit sky. It was almost as if she could take in only one visual stimulus at a time and had to savour and evaluate it before allowing herself to move on to the next.

She turned to Kelvin, who was looking anxiously at her. 'Get me a sherry,' she said.

We considered her request. Crisp, clear, to the point and no messing about. She knew what she wanted and asked for it. Kelvin went over to try to find a sherry as she stood placidly by the fire, her legs slightly apart, examining the sizzling sausages rather hungrily. She seemed perfectly content just to stand and cogitate on the grilling pigmeat, but her self-possession and calm created a little circle of disturbance. It was as if a bacterium had invaded the bloodstream and the white corpuscles were twitching and heaving about, wondering quite what they ought to do about it.

Dennis, bless his heart, took it upon himself to try to integrate her into the party. He approached her with an ingratiating smile wreathed across his lips. Conversation, which had begun to start up again after the initial impact of the couple's arrival, died away again as we all stretched our ears to hear the exchange. As Dennis walked towards her, she turned her head and looked at him warily, as if she expected him to turn somersaults or do something equally unexpected.

'Good evening. My name is Dennis. I'm a friend of Kelvin's. Er . . . Welcome to the village.' She continued to look stolidly at him. 'Er . . . Do you come from round here?'

We appreciated the question. It would not do to embarrass her by making her think we had been talking about her or knew too much about her.

'No,' she replied. Dennis smiled at her encouragingly, but it appeared that she had nothing more to say on the subject. He took a hurried gulp of his whisky as Kelvin lurched over to join them, bearing a couple of glasses of wine.

'Evening, Dennis.'

'Evening, Kelvin.'

'Good party, innit?'

'Yes,' replied Dennis. 'I was just talking to your companion.'

'Oh? What about?' Kelvin seemed desperately eager to find out.

'We hadn't actually got very far. I was just introducing myself, but your friend hasn't yet told me her name.'

Something seemed to stir deep behind the lady's eyes and she looked as if she was about to speak, but Kelvin clumsily destroyed the magic of the moment before she had time to sift through all the considerations and actually commit herself to utterance.

''Course you know her name. She's Matilda from London. The one that sent the letter. Who else do you think I'd bring along here?'

Dennis raised his eyes to the stars in exasperation. Lindy saw the difficulty that Kelvin's obtuseness was creating in the search for information, and so she went across to lend a hand. Dennis flashed her a look of gratitude. There was nothing else that Lindy could be except the district nurse: she looked so capable with her short hair, square, strong hands and air of being able to handle all the nasties that life might throw at her and come bouncing back for more. She donned her bedside manner which put at ease her most awkward patients.

'Hullo. What a lovely dress.' She paused for a split second, realized that she was not going to get an answer and carried smoothly on. 'Where did you manage to find it?'

A slight look of alarm crossed Matilda's face as she swivelled her head towards Lindy. The hush as she opened her mouth was almost palpable. 'Don't remember.'

'Oh, come on,' said Lindy encouragingly. 'You must remember where you bought a lovely dress like that.'

'A present, it was.'

'How nice! And who gave it to you?'

'I can't remember.'

The conversation, as Lindy put it later, was like taking out stitches. She and Kelvin were studying Matilda's face, willing her to utter, while Dennis had given up and was trying to solve the conundrum of her breasts under the guise of studying the bottom of his whisky glass. It was not made easy by the flickering light of the fire which forced him to lean down and squint a bit. Lindy girded her loins and moved back into the conversational fray.

'How long are you here for?'

'Dunno,' replied Matilda. 'It depends.'

Lindy looked across at Kelvin for some help. A look of panic crossed his face and he hurriedly backed away, moving over to where Bill and the commander were standing surveying Matilda.

'Did you come down from London?' continued Lindy doggedly.

'That's right. On a train. From Paddington.' She paused again and then suddenly spoke, making both Lindy and Dennis jump. 'It took ever such a short time and that gentleman was waiting for me at the station.' She indicated Kelvin. She delved into her handbag and produced a small piece of paper which she studied carefully. Dennis tried to read it too, but it was upside down. She grinned. She was one of those rare people who look less attractive when they smile. 'Kelvin, that's what he's called. He's ever so nice although he's quite old.' She sank her voice to a whisper as all and sundry strained their ears to hear and there was complete silence, except for the yelp of a dog as someone sank their foot into its ribs to stop it making the night hideous with its scratching. 'He might offer me a job. He's a very important man round here, you know. He used to be a very senior policeman and they asked him if he would be the local mayor, or something, but he said he was too busy. Everyone in the district is very jealous of him because he's so popular.'

'Is that right?' said Lindy. 'What else did he tell you?'

'Oh, I shouldn't go round repeating confidences. That's one thing I told Kelvin. I never gossip. I don't believe in that sort of thing.'

'You're absolutely right,' said Dennis. 'Gossip is a terrible thing and it's easy to see that you're the sort of person who never gossips about other people. Isn't it, Lindy?'

Lindy nodded assent.

'Oh! Is your name Lindy?' asked Matilda.

'That's right.'

'What a coincidence! Kelvin was talking about someone called Lindy earlier on.'

'Really?' said Lindy. 'That must be the district nurse. She's called Lindy, just the same as me. What did he say about her?'

'I shouldn't say, really.'

'No, of course you shouldn't,' said Dennis, perceiving minefields ahead.

'— But he said she was very bossy.'

'Oh, did he?' said Lindy grimly. One couldn't help hoping that Kelvin would never need an enema. Others at the party had begun to close in on Matilda, desirous of overhearing further indiscretions. Ivor did the gentlemanly thing and made sure that Kelvin's attention was fully occupied by bringing up some query about communications after the atomic holocaust. This was Kelvin's current obsession since he had taken over the planning of the parish's survival after the bomb had dropped. When he was safely out of earshot, Lindy did not so much have to pump Matilda as pull out her plug.

'He's awfully clever, that Kelvin, and a very shrewd businessman, you know.'

'In what way?' cooed Lindy.

'He was saying that there was some old lady who owned a small bit of land at the edge of the churchyard and he went and bought it very cheaply the other day, because he knows that they'll have to buy it when they want some more room and he'll be able to name his own price. Isn't that clever?'

There was a stunned silence. It had come up in a meeting of the parochial church council a few weeks earlier that the graveyard was getting a bit crowded and that something would have to be done about it. Kelvin, being a heathen, was not a member, but he must have heard someone mention it in the pub.

It was evident that Matilda was far too precious an insertion into the shady areas of Kelvin's soul to be allowed to vanish back to her urban rookery and Lindy and Dennis left her in the capable hands of the commander while they went to join Ivor in his distraction display.

'What a splendid woman, Kelvin. You are a lucky chap,' was Dennis's greeting.

Ivor looked startled, while Kelvin examined Dennis suspiciously to try to establish whether or not the mickey was being taken out of him.

'Yes. She seems awfully nice,' echoed Lindy.

Kelvin peered at her in turn. 'Do you really think so? I was wondering if she might not be all that bright. I'm not sure that I could stand her round the farm all day.'

'Not all that bright?' said Dennis in amazement. 'I thought she was very bright. Didn't you, Lindy?'

Lindy corroborated with a vigorous nod of her head. 'Certainly. She may not be in line for a double first at Oxford, but she's certainly sharp enough. And witty.'

'Witty!' said Kelvin. 'I haven't heard her crack many jokes. Come to think on it, I've hardly heard her say anything at all.'

'Really? Well, I find her very witty.' Lindy emitted a peal of laughter to show how witty Matilda was. It was so unlike her usual earthy chuckle that Kelvin and Dennis gave her a startled look. She tried another peal and managed to produce a more normal sound.

'Hmm,' said Kelvin. 'I'm not sure that I want to live in the same house as someone who cracks jokes the whole time.'

'She's not *that* funny,' said Lindy, rather more scathingly than was appropriate.

'Certainly not,' agreed Dennis. 'Just about right. Witty without being tedious. I would have thought that she was exactly the sort of person that you should be looking for.'

Kelvin rubbed his chin thoughtfully. 'Well, I have to admit she's pretty near to it, but don't you think she's a little plain? She's not as pretty as the photograph she sent.'

'I think she's very pretty,' replied Dennis gallantly. 'And her most impressive features certainly live up to expectations.'

'I agree,' said Lindy. 'You agree too, don't you, Ivor?'

Ivor jumped. 'Oh yes, quite.' He was a little bemused, not understanding why Matilda should have gathered such a devoted fan club so quickly.

'Do you really think so?' said Kelvin. 'What about that jaw of hers?'

Lindy was having some difficulty in stomaching this cold dissection of Matilda. She may also have been harbouring doubts about the morality of this exercise in manipulation. At any rate, she let her mask of goodwill slip a little. 'You're a fine one to start criticizing Matilda,' she snapped.

'I think her jaw is fine – most beguiling,' said Dennis hastily, frowning at Lindy. If one started to prod at the great tottering blancmange that was Kelvin's vanity, he could become unmanageable. Fortunately, his hearing was highly selective and he chose to ignore Lindy's remark.

'Hmm,' said Kelvin, but he looked happier than he had done when he had first arrived at the party and he went over to top up Matilda's drink. The obvious appreciation of his contemporaries had burnished up her appeal in his eyes and he stood by her side for the rest of the evening, looking on with slightly puzzled pride as the villagers, one by one at Dennis's prompting, went up and made manifest how delightful they all found Matilda to be.

We had underestimated Matilda. Ivor met her on the platform of the station on Monday morning. He was going up for a Milk Marketing Board meeting and she was going home. Kelvin had offered her the job and had indicated that it could lead to a great deal more, but Matilda had not been seduced by the idea of becoming his housekeeper and still less had she been willing to be seduced by the man himself.

'A miserable old bastard,' was her pithy summing up. 'I'm better off with my husband.'

It was a pity, but we quite understood her point of view. She walked off with £500 as well. Kelvin could not report it as he had not declared it to the Inland Revenue. The sympathy he received was underwhelming.

Chapter Nine

'YOU KNOW HOW we country people are different from those who live in towns, don't you?' asked Muriel, carefully measuring another couple of inches of gin into her glass.

'God! She's going to get boring again,' replied her sister Barbara.

'Do shut up, dear. It's because we need to make money through our own initiative. In towns all you have to do is go out and work for someone else. Out here, nobody gives you money. You have to go and get it for yourself.'

We were sitting round their kitchen table at 10.30 in the morning. It was hard work visiting the sisters. Whatever time of the day or night, one was never offered tea or coffee, but only alcohol. They drank gin while visitors were offered cooking sherry. This was an economy measure. Most visitors never touched or never finished the vast drinks that were pressed upon them and it hurt less to pour bad sherry down the drain than good gin.

The sisters were both widows and bickered furiously with each other. Muriel had taken me aside once to tell me what lay at the foundation of their disagreements: 'I was the clever one when we were girls and I had curly hair. Barbara was stupid and had straight hair and so she was very jealous of me. And she has never got over it.'

Muriel had married a sailor and had produced a stream of amiably unsuccessful children whom she despised. Barbara had married a colonial judge who had died of a heart attack the day the unthinkable had happened and his colony had achieved its independence. When they reached their seventies, they had come together again to continue the ritual they had begun in childhood of being extremely rude to each other and the ritual they had adopted in adulthood of spending as many of their waking moments as possible in a state that would have melted the bottom of a breathalyser bag.

I had called to return the tortoise. It had come with the house which had been an old smithy at the edge of the village. The reptile had been there the ten years that the sisters had been living there and a yellowing photograph showed the animal beside the last blacksmith. Its name, Bleriot, indicated that it had probably been around for the best part of a century. The creature was even mentioned in the house deeds as part of the fixtures and fittings of the establishment, but nobody had asked the tortoise whether it approved of the arrangement. It had dug itself into the rose-bed one winter and, when it woke up in the spring, it had a new owner. It had been rudely disturbed by Muriel's Afghan which had been in the process of burying a bone.

The Afghan had only been a puppy then, but it had been love at first sight. The dog's idea of a blissfully consummated relationship was to go for a long country walk with the freaked-out tortoise, frantically waving its legs, firmly clasped between its jaws. There was never a problem when they met other dogs. After a brief examination of the block-mouthed, growling Jellicoe, one could see them dismiss him with the thought of 'nutter'.

Bleriot decided early on that the best solution to his difficulties lay in emigrating and, whenever Jellicoe was not concentrating, he would plod grimly down the garden path and head south towards a better world. Unfortunately for him, his route took him past our front door and he would invariably be fielded by ourselves, by Jellicoe in a lather of panicked excitement, or by a motorist, happy enough to flatten hedgehogs but unwilling to risk his tyres or suspension on a large tortoise.

On this occasion, I had given the reptile twenty-four hours of peace amid our lettuces before returning it to its rightful owners and having to undergo the obligatory sherry. The sisters were arguing as usual when I came through the door and they both gave me imperious – if unfocused – glances as I entered.

'Thank you,' said Barbara, graciously accepting the errant creature. 'Such a pity they're inedible, isn't it?'

'Barbara! How could you! Poor Bleriot.'

Poor Bleriot was looking as if his consumption would have been a merciful release. He was lying underneath the kitchen table, upside down, firmly anchored beneath Jellicoe's paw, while the dog was peering earnestly into his shell, slapping his face with a long pink tongue whenever he dared to poke it out. I rose to leave, abandoning the latter half of my sherry.

'Oh yes,' said Barbara as I moved towards the door. She turned round in her chair, overbalanced and slid to the ground.

'Shit,' she said, but continued from the floor: 'We are looking for a way of earning some more money. It would be appreciated if you would come up with some ideas.'

A tallish order, off the back foot, I thought.

Muriel looked at me hopefully. 'The trouble is that our expenses are so high. We have certain little luxuries to which we have become accustomed.' She carefully topped up her gin from the litre bottle on the table in front of her. Her speech and her bleary gaze gave the impression that she was on the point of collapse, but the iron grip with which she held the bottle was as steady as that of a surgeon scrabbling around amid someone's brains.

‘How about buying your little luxuries wholesale?’ I suggested. Mick at the cafe had a daily delivery run, supplying spirits by the crate-load to the army of retired who lived in the village and the surrounding countryside. He charged full retail prices and slapped on a whacking delivery charge. A significant proportion of the pensions paid out by the Ministry of Defence and the civil service must eventually end up in the glens of the Scottish Highlands and in their distilleries.

‘Buy wholesale? But how would we pick it up?’ asked Barbara. That was the ‘Catch-22’ which was enabling Mick to get rich. From 10.00 am to midnight, most of those over sixty-five in the district were well beyond the legal driving limit. ‘No, we want to earn money. Quite apart from anything else, it would give us something to do.’

‘Are you serious?’ I asked.

‘Well, fairly serious. We wouldn’t want to do anything strenuous. There’s our 10-acre field out the back, for example. There must be something more profitable that we can do with it than just rent it out to Dick Hunniford so he can cover it with his sheep.’

‘Cover it with your own sheep. That’s got to be more profitable.’

‘Don’t be so stupid. I am willing to look at sheep from my bedroom window and I am even prepared to eat selected parts of the creatures, but I have no desire to become more closely involved with such a moronic species of animal. You can run along now.’

So I ran along.

A couple of weeks later, there was a bit of excitement in the village. An enormous yellow bulldozer was seen crabbing its way down the side of one of the hills that surrounded us. Such visitations were uncommon. The narrow lanes kept out most heavy vehicles. It was a blessing in many respects, until an ignorant driver managed to penetrate as far as the village itself when he would get himself into an inextricable articulated tangle at the corner of the pub and the post office, while Land Rovers and horseboxes backed up for half a mile on either side of him. It brought out the beast in Percy when he tried to sort it out.

Bulldozers roamed the countryside on the back of huge flat-bed lorries, grubbing out hedges and scouring the bottom of slurry pits wherever they stopped. Their lorry would get them as close to their destination as possible and then they set off by themselves in a bee-line to wherever they wished to go. Oddly enough, although there was plenty of sound and fury as they travelled and it looked as though their tracks would leave great tramlines slashed across the landscape, once the belching, roaring machine had disappeared over the horizon, there would be a tingling silence; the crushed vegetation and saplings would cautiously unfold themselves and, within a couple of hours, it was as if the machine had never passed.

The bulldozer on this particular visitation clanked its way to the bottom of the hill, cautiously edged its way into the river and gingerly crossed through the summer-low water before triumphantly snorting its way out on the far side and climbing into Barbara and Muriel's field. What on earth was going on?

The jungle drums muttered and rumbled in their quest for intelligence, but none of the usual sources could come up with any information. The machine crunched to a halt by the edge of the stream that ran down the centre of the precipitous field, and its operator disembarked and walked over to the house. The watchers – not twitching their lace curtains so much as standing in the fields and their gardens with binoculars clamped to their eyes – relaxed, knowing that the driver would now be sitting at the kitchen table with a tumblerful of cheap sherry in front of him and would soon be incapable of any further work for the day.

However, within an hour, people tumbled out of their houses again as an echoing blare bounced round the valley to announce that the jaundiced behemoth had restarted its engine. It was rootling about with its blade on the bed of the stream, was the report: digging a pond, clearly.

That did not last long. The water authority was inundated with calls from local citizens who felt it their duty to ascertain that proper permission had been obtained for such action and

Ivor, in his role of parish councillor, turned up on the smithy doorstep to advise Barbara and Muriel that it was in their interest to halt the work until the proper permission had been obtained. It took some time to sort out the red tape and it took some time for Ivor to recover from the effects of having a tortoise bounced off his head, but work eventually restarted.

The sisters had permission to dig out a large pond, fed by the stream, into which they were going to place rainbow trout. These were to be caught by visiting anglers who would be charged by the pound, at a higher rate than the fish would cost them if purchased from a fishmonger. It was quite a bright idea, another neat method of separating the tourists from their money.

The bulldozer roared and puffed for a week. Barbara supervised for a day and then had to delegate to Muriel after she had annoyed the driver to such an extent that he chased her round the field, trying to swat her with the blade of his machine.

When the work was completed, it had all the charm of a bomb site. It formed a massive scar on the hillside which was glaringly obvious as one came along the road leading to the bridge into the village. Its colour was what created the eyesore: most of the valley was a vivid grass-green, but the bulldozer had dragged up the subsoil which was clay in blue and yellow layers and had piled it up to dam the stream. Right in the centre of this garish protuberance was an ominous band of grey.

This band gave rise to problems. It was good porous shale, through which the stream continued to chuckle its merry way down to the river, refusing, with complete self-assurance, even to consider spreading itself across the carefully prepared floor of the pond which remained sparsely and sullenly puddled. The delivery of trout was postponed and I, returning Bleriot yet again, was called in to advise.

I had the reputation of being quite an expert at this sort of thing, having spent a few years of my life trying to persuade a slurry pit to leak gently and economically into the environment and thus save me the expense of having to hire a bulldozer to empty it. However, this was a reversal of my accustomed role and I was not sure that my experience was up to stopping flows rather than encouraging them.

I managed to avoid more than a single sip of sherry, Jellicoe emptying my glass while Barbara's back was turned. We walked out through the glass door that led from the kitchen into the garden where I carefully placed the tortoise in the middle of the lawn and watched him for a second or two until he collected himself and began to plod determinedly back towards the gate that led into the lane. The garden halted abruptly about 10 yards from the smithy and became a 4-foot-high expanse of nettles – 'The nature reserve,' said Barbara airily, as we raised our arms above our heads and cautiously waded through the alien, sour smell of the crushed plants marking our progress.

'You're going to have to make some sort of an entrance for the fishermen,' I said. 'You can't have them wading through this lot.'

'All in good time.'

We reached the fence by the edge of the field. Already it had changed its character. Gone was the St Andrews-quality fairway that had been created by the tenant sheep, their cropping keeping the grass down to a springy couple of inches. The animals had been evicted before the arrival of the bulldozer and the field was in danger of becoming an extension of the nature reserve with thistles, docks, nettles and buttercups seizing the opportunity to spring up to compete with the rank grass for air space. We walked across to the edge of the pond.

'Well, there seems to be a decent flow of water,' I said, watching the stream as it gurgled across the pond and disappeared into the wall, emerging, like magic, on the other side.

'I can see that,' said Barbara, scathingly. 'But it's supposed to fill the pond rather than go straight across. How do I stop it?'

I was a bit wary. I had a feeling that plugging leaks in ponds might be a bit like hammering a nail into a brick wall – something that led to much heartache and little success. I was not sure that I wanted to take on this particular responsibility.

'There are several things you could try,' I said non-committally.

'Yes. We've thought of trying to spread clay over the shale, or putting down a sheet of butyl rubber or even a sheet of polythene.'

'Yes. That's the sort of thing I would have recommended.'

'Which do you think would be best?'

'Well, they all have certain points in their favour. What would they all cost?'

'The clay puddling would be cheapest in itself, but it would probably mean bringing back the bulldozer to make a decent job of it.' Barbara must have had lengthy periods of sobriety recently to collate this sort of information. 'That would cost quite a lot. The rubber is meant to be jolly good, but it's expensive too and that just leaves the plastic.'

'It sounds like the plastic, then.'

'Do you really think so? I had come to that conclusion as

well. After all, it's not likely that water will be able to get through polythene.'

I was not quite so sure. Polythene was all very well, in my experience, until it got a hole in it, and it only took one wasp in a filthy temper to make a hole.

'You will come and help lay it, won't you?' asked Barbara.

The sisters did not waste much time. An immense roll of black agricultural polythene was dumped outside their front gate a couple of days later and I was ordered to assist with the laying thereof that afternoon. There were three of us, Frank Mattock who farmed up behind the smithy and whose land bordered the field, the commander and myself.

The commander was still a bit of an agricultural virgin in spite of his market garden, and it soon showed. 'Let's get that polythene off the road, first,' he said, marching up to the roll of plastic and bending down to pick up one end.

'Hang on a minute, Commander,' said Frank, but it was too late. The commander grasped the roll and tried to lift it. Half-way up, his face turned white. He then sank back to his knees, put the plastic down and rested his hands on the ground. Jellicoe and the sisters had come out to greet their workforce and the dog went up to the commander and started to lick his face. Barbara looked at him suspiciously. He appeared to be deep in prayer, facing Mecca, and was ignoring Jellicoe whose tongue must have smelled of tortoise if not of his own intimate orifices.

'Are you all right?' asked Muriel.

'I think I'm going to be sick,' came the faint reply.

'Don't be silly,' said Barbara.

'I'm fairly sure I'm going to be sick.'

Barbara bent down and tried to examine the commander's face.

'Good Lord! I do believe the fellow's pissed. How utterly lamentable!'

Frank and I looked at her in astonishment and even the commander wearily turned his head and tried to see her through the spray of Jellicoe's saliva. It was a superb example of the pot calling the kettle black, but she appeared unconscious of the irony.

'I'm not drunk,' said the commander in a strained voice. 'I've just put my back out.'

'Nonsense,' boomed Barbara. 'You're just a bloody shirker.'

A vague pink wash of incipient fury suffused the commander's cheeks, but an attempt to rise to his feet rapidly drained this flicker of life from his face and he sank back to his knees with a moan. Frank and I were sympathetic. For the male sex, no pain can equal that moment of exquisite, pure agony which you experience when you first put your back out. Break a leg, be mauled by a puma, and the shock of the injury masks the pain, but there is no natural anaesthetic when the back goes. And it is a pain that almost every working countryman has had to live through. The commander began to giggle.

'Christ! It must be bad,' said Frank.

'It's bad,' agreed the commander. The giggle is a well-known reaction to the onset of severe back trouble. It is the origin of the saying 'If I don't laugh, I'll cry' at the sheer outrage to the nervous system.

'Humph,' said Barbara, striding over to the commander,

kicking Jellicoe out of the way as she approached. 'Let me give you a hand up.'

'Get away from me,' said the sufferer, as he fought to control his laughter. It is not funny when you start to laugh when your back goes. You want to be utterly still to minimize the pain and the last thing you need is for your belly and your diaphragm to start heaving about. 'Just leave me alone, please,' he begged.

'But we can't leave you on your hands and knees in the middle of the road,' said Barbara.

'Yes, you can. The bloody tortoise can walk round me.'

We left him to his agony. It apparently took him half an hour to recover sufficiently to move, another half-hour to walk home, and then his wife made the fatal mistake of persuading him to take to his bed. With that degree of back trouble, if you take to your bed, you are liable to stay there forever. The only cure is to force yourself to your feet and keep moving.

With the commander out of action, Frank and I carefully picked up either end of the plastic roll while the ladies supported the middle and we all tottered round the side of the smithy into the field where the pond lay. It was like carrying a cannon: every undulation of the ground made us stagger off course as we fought against gravity and the random forces exerted by the ladies. We came to the pond and, while the ladies bickered as to the best place to put down the burden, Frank and I pre-empted them by dropping it with a toe-crunching thud.

The pond had potential. It was a good size – about 30 yards by 50 with a thistle-covered island carefully left by the bulldozer, slightly off-centre to allow the stream to flow past on the starboard side. With a slight effort, one could imagine the clay covered by rippling water, damsel flies flitting round the vegetation of the water margin and rings left by the rising trout. But all that required a leak-proof bed and, at that moment, the pond was a desolation of blue and yellow clay.

'I suggest,' said Barbara, confidently, 'that we place the roll of plastic on the dam wall and just unroll it upstream to the edge of the pond.'

I had forgotten my gumboots, but it was a warm and sunny day and there were worse ways of passing it than dabbling around in water with squidgy clay oozing between my toes.

Frank had not yet understood the basis on which he had been recruited. 'I'm not sure that starting down here would be the best way, Barbara. If we unroll it from the top, it would be a damn sight easier and the water would be less likely to get under the sheet.'

'Don't argue with me,' said Barbara with tight-lipped patience. 'Just do what I say, please, Frank.'

Barbara still lived in those legendary golden days of yesteryear when the lower orders knew their place while the gentry benignly cared for them, saving them from the folly of their feckless ways, and all that was asked in return was a slavish subservience. Frank was helping out for nothing. He could have bought her out without even having to tug his forelock in the direction of the bank manager and, whereas Barbara's knowledge of the behaviour of liquids was confined to the 75cl within the average bottle of spirits, Frank farmed many acres within a 65-inch rainfall belt. The effective control and disposal of water was as important a part of his job as being able to tell the difference between a sheep and a cow. For a few seconds, I thought he might tell Barbara precisely what she could do with her roll of polythene, but then he caught my eye and winked.

'If that's the way you want it, Missus. But remember, I can only help you today. I start combining tomorrow.'

'That's the way I want it,' replied Barbara.

So we began to unroll the sheet and carefully spread the polythene over the shale on the bank up to the level of a drainage pipe that had been laid to take care of the overflow. Then we ran it up the stream across the floor of the pond up to the point where it shelved back into the field; in theory, the stream was now running over a waterproof plastic bed. It took less than half an hour.

'Right,' said Barbara. 'That was very easy. Thank you so much.'

'May I make a suggestion?' said Frank.

'Certainly,' responded Barbara graciously.

'It might be a good idea to dig the edges of the sheet into the clay to provide a watertight seal.'

'You worry too much, Frank. It won't be necessary. The water is not going to get underneath the sheet.'

'Whatever you say. But remember, I'm combining for the rest of the week.'

'I'll remember,' replied Barbara patiently, and we walked back to the smithy to be given a glass of sherry – finest British ruby sweet oloroso – in payment for our services.

At 10.00 am the following morning, Barbara summoned me. She was not in a good mood. There was quite a respectable puddle on the plastic underneath the dam wall – at least as big as the shubunkin pool in front of Mandyandkeith's – but the pond ought to have been virtually full and even spilling out through the overflow by this time.

'There are obviously holes in the sheet. It's a scandal that they should supply faulty goods like this.'

'It strikes me that it's far more likely that the water is going under the sheet.'

'Nonsense.'

'Barbara, if you look, you will observe that the water is running down the polythene very nicely and spreading out until it comes to the edge. Then it spreads no further. For heaven's sake, the sheet of plastic is even floating at the edge.'

Barbara looked. 'Humph! I suppose it is possible. What's to be done?'

'Frank suggested digging the sheet into the clay.'

'Oh no. There's no need to go to all that trouble. It just needs a few stones round the edge to hold it down and stop it floating.'

'I doubt if that will do the trick.'

'Of course it will.'

Of course it did not. Barbara and Muriel spent much of the day trundling rocks across the bed of the pond and placing them so that they anchored the sheet. I was dismissed for being insufficiently positive in my thinking, but was recalled the next morning when it had become obvious that Frank's advice would have to be followed. The first task was to remove all the rocks that had been placed by the sisters the day before. I was aided by a grumbling Barbara while Muriel, who was slightly better at winning friends and influencing people, went into the village to try to rustle up some labour.

The Grabber, whom she had cornered in the post office while he was posting his pools entry, was all she could come up with. Nobody else was in a position to drop everything and come running in order to be cursed by Barbara.

The Grabber, who had earned his nickname through his behaviour at barn dances in his youth, was a hedge-layer, and he had been able to make a very good living at it. It was still an important skill in the village which was surrounded by mile after mile of great hedge banks, taking up a disproportionate amount of agricultural land. These banks had been established a thousand years ago by the pioneers who had first cleared the land round about in order to grow their crops. Stones and boulders had been laboriously prised out of the ground and piled up in neat rows where it had been decided to make the field boundaries. Over the centuries, these walls had grown over and become hedges, completely stockproof and giving shelter to the animals like no barbed-wire fence ever could. The old craftsmen had proved to be more perishable than their landscape. Men like the Grabber could approach a neglected hedge, crowned by a spindly line of 20-foot saplings through which both wind and sheep could pass without impediment, and transform it with a few strokes of the billhook into a tight, living barrier of woven branches, once again providing shelter to a score of species of animals and birds.

During the previous decade, the price applicable to the piecework of hedge laying had risen spectacularly since the skills needed for the job were disappearing much faster than the hedges themselves. An untrained layer would take twice as long as the Grabber, and those of his ilk, to do the job and the rate had to be high enough to persuade the non-specialist to take on the work. So both the Grabber and the local pub had grown prosperous.

Then the Grabber had been asked to do a job on the family farm. The farm, operated by a cousin, had been owned by the family since the days of the Tudors. Our part of the country had never attracted the great barons who bought up or expropriated vast tracts of land which they parcelled out to their feudal retainers. We were too far from the centre of power in London and the land was not good enough. So we had a tradition of independent yeoman farmers, each with 100–200 acres, who did not need to bow down to anyone.

Such farmers tended to take a long view of their business and the Grabber's family was no exception. On the farm, there was one 10-acre patch that had been allowed to revert to scrubland. This patch seemed to have gone in and out of production as circumstances demanded since it had first been cleared by the Grabber's Saxon forebears. Its recent history had been recorded. It had grown wheat during the Napoleonic Wars and was then left alone until the 1860s when it had grown potatoes. It became scrub again until the First World War, when it was growing oats, and was left to its own devices during the Depression of the nineteen-thirties until the Second World War, when it had grown barley. When the civil servants of the War Agricultural Commission had returned to their offices, it had been allowed to revert once again.

The Grabber's cousin decided to bring this piece of land back into production as he wished to expand his beef herd, and the Grabber was called in to tame the hedges and re-hang the gates while the trees, which had crept over the couple of fields that were there, were being cleared.

Then problems had arisen. A retired architect, who wrote a column called 'Mother Nature's News' for a group of local newspapers in the Midlands, had heard about the plans and had lobbied against them so successfully that the 10 acres had been designated a Site of Special Scientific Interest with the result that nobody was to be allowed to farm them ever again. In vain was it pleaded that there was nothing natural about the few acres. They had been thoroughly farmed, albeit on and off, for a millennium and the ancient hedgerows were there to prove it. Even if the land was cleared, there was little doubt that it would revert back to bog and scrubby woodland after a decade or two. All that made it botanically interesting was the frequent change in the type of habitat that it provided and that specialness would be destroyed if it was decided to fossilize the site in such an arbitrary way.

The decree was passed, however. The bemused farmer was offered a management agreement which undertook to pay him a certain sum of money in perpetuity provided that he left that corner of the farm alone. The Grabber was disgusted and hung up his billhook for good. As he had said, what was the point of trying to do a decent job any more, if any ignorant booby could come along and tell you to ruin the land and even pay you good money to do it? The Grabber had retired to his cabbages, his courgettes, his cider and his post as assistant verger at the church, but he still liked to keep his hand in, and was always willing to join in anything that was going on, so he was delighted to answer Muriel's call for aid.

The sisters had only one spade which I used, but the Grabber had brought his fork and we worked our way round the edge of the sheet. It was rather satisfying, a bit like digging peat, as the spade slipped easily into the clay to remove a neat, brick-shaped clod. We carefully dug a shallow trench all the way round the sheet into which we placed the edges of the polythene before replacing the clods and carefully treading them in. It was a three-hour job but, by the end of it, the bed of the pond was well and truly watertight. There was nothing now to prevent the sisters ordering a tankload of silvery trout which could be tumbled into the pool from the back of a Land Rover and their bonanza could begin.

The Grabber and I went to sit on the island to watch the stream, frustrated in its attempts to escape, sullenly start to spread itself over the edge of the sheet and across the base of the pond. Barbara and Muriel came to join us, bearing a couple of deckchairs and cider as a more appropriate drink for labourers who had completed their allotted task than the customary gin or sherry.

'I'd really like to thank you both for all your work,' said Muriel.

'To tell the truth I was quite glad to get away from the garden,' replied the Grabber. 'It makes a bit of a change. Now that I'm an old man, I don't get out that much.'

'You're an old fraud, Grabber,' I said. 'You're in the pub

twice a day and you follow every pack of hounds within a 20-mile radius.'

The Grabber shook his head with a sigh. 'No, I don't follow the hunt these days. I suppose it's because I'm getting on and I'm happy now to let all God's creatures live in peace. I don't hold with hunting like I used to.'

'For heaven's sake,' I exclaimed, 'you sound just like Walter Gabriel!'

'Leave the old boy alone,' said Barbara, ignoring the fact that he was ten years younger than her. 'I know exactly how he feels. When you get to our age, life becomes precious and you learn to live from day to day. I used to hunt when I was a big younger, but I wouldn't dream of it now. I like to see living things around me.'

This lump-in-the-throat stuff, coming from two of the most outrageously hard-boiled characters in the community, was too much to endure. I was not going to let them get away with it, particularly Barbara. 'If life is so sacred now that you are in your dotage, Barbara, why are you encouraging tourists to lure your fish to their doom?'

Barbara sighed and was echoed by the Grabber with whom she exchanged a glance that pitied my lack of understanding. 'Don't think that it is by choice. We are often forced into situations that we regret by economic circumstances. I wish there had been another way, but Muriel and I have to live.'

Muriel poured us another drink out of a gallon plastic container. It was rough farmhouse scrumpy – so rough that the label was not even printed, but hand-written. She had brought out a picnic lunch of bread and cheese and Scotch eggs which she passed round. I lay on my back, listening to the sound of the stream and watching the tiny dots of the larks against the blue of the sky. 'Oh look! There's a rat,' said Muriel.

'What?' I asked, not really listening, since I was trying to calculate the mean speed of skylark droppings when they hit the ground if released from a height of 200 feet.

'Look. Over there. There's a rat.'

I propped myself up on my elbow. So there was. It was a young rat, half-grown – because no adult rodent would be stupid enough to walk about in the middle of the day in full view of a group of people. It was sniffing around on the highly unpromising territory of the bed of the pond. It was rather sweet, really.

Barbara put down the newspaper she had been reading and looked over the top of her spectacles. She looked and she saw. She sank her foot into the dozing Grabber's ribs. He sat up, rubbed the sleep from his eyes and looked round and saw.

'Bloody hell!' said the Grabber. He struggled to his feet, snatched up his fork and plunged down the bank of the island in pursuit. The rat stopped sniffing and watched him come, waving his fork and uttering inarticulate cries. It was a very laid-back rodent. It allowed him to get within 10 yards before it decided that the Grabber might not be a dedicated member of the League Against Cruel Sports and so it turned and ambled off across the pond. The Grabber steamed after it while Barbara, now on her feet, jumped up and down with excitement.

'Kill it! Go on, kill it!' she shrieked.

The Grabber was doing his best. He had virtually caught up with the rat which was still showing a remarkably casual attitude to the business of its own survival. Perhaps it realized that the Grabber was still dazed by sleep and cider and not much of a threat. He was plunging his fork again and again into the ground, trying to spear the animal, but his aim was lousy.

The rat reached the stream and paused with its pursuer only a yard or two behind. Muriel closed her eyes so that she would not have to witness the bloody deed. I watched in resigned fascination while Barbara continued to scream encouragement. There was no need to worry. The animal placed its paw delicately in the water, decided that it was too cold and turned, scuttling between the Grabber's legs, and wandered off up the side of the stream to disappear in the long grass at the pond's edge. The Grabber puffed his way back to the island.

'Bad luck,' said Barbara. 'That was jolly exciting. You very nearly got it.'

The Grabber collapsed on the grass. 'Blooming heck. I haven't run like that for years. D'you see the little bugger jink? He was a right fly one, that. I reckon someone must have chased him before.'

Muriel still had her eyes closed and was now muttering a prayer for strength and patience beneath her breath. So I took it upon myself to break the bad news.

'There's just one problem, Grabber.'

'Oh yes?'

'The watertight plastic sheet. I would guess, conservatively, that it now has about a hundred fork holes in it.'

The Grabber and Barbara stared out over the bed of the pond. There was a rumbling sound from Barbara and the volcano burst. Muriel and I clapped our hands over our ears while people throughout the village anxiously inspected the sky for thunderclouds.

'You unbelievably stupid old fart!' she bellowed. 'You've ruined it!'

'You were encouraging me.'

Muriel and I left them to it and walked back to the smithy. I made sure that I was not around when the sheet was removed and the shale was covered in a layer of clay.

Chapter Ten

IT WAS KELVIN who coined the expression 'swallows'. Swallows were the people who came to live in the village and the surrounding area who had not actually been born there. The typical swallow was a thrusting young executive and his wife who would buy a cottage, do it up, live in it for a few years and then find that the education of their children, or the demands of his career, or even the mind-boggling boredom of having to mix with country bumpkins at the weekends, meant that they had to sell up and move on to somewhere else. Swallows flitted prettily about the community for a season or two without putting down roots and migrated on to sunnier climes.

The Jarretts were the epitome of the swallow. They had bought an extremely rough cottage in River Lane, a couple of doors down from Mandyandkeith, for a price that had still been the talk of the country estate agents' annual dinner-dance a couple of years later. They had then gutted it, removing what few period charms it may have possessed, and converted its interior into a fine example of High Islington Camp.

They had little to do with the village at first. In their thirties, they were both small and pretty and they commuted to teaching jobs in the market town on the back of a huge Japanese motorcycle, wearing matching scarlet overalls and crash helmets.

Then, during their first summer, on one of those still, warm evenings when the swifts screamed through the streets and even the yawn of a stretching dog seemed to echo off the front of the cottages, the sound of loud rock music was heard emerging through their Georgian-style windows. Jimmy had craned his neck to look in as he made his delicately septuagenarian way up to the pub. He had not been quite able to make out what the Jarretts were up to, but they weren't sitting in front of an organ like Mandy had been.

'All I could see was two arses poking in the air.'

'Were they on top of each other, Jimmy?' Kelvin had asked.

'No, I can't say that they were. More side by side.'

'That's a bit strange. Side by side and not on top of each other. Especially on a Sunday evening,' chuckled Billy. He worked as a mechanic in the local garage and fancied himself as the local Lothario.

'Not everyone's like you, Billy,' said Kelvin.

'I bet they wish they were,' replied Billy, with the self-satisfied macho smirk of the inadequate cocksman trying to reassure himself that he was otherwise. Jimmy shot him a look of distaste before continuing. The art of successful gossip lies in delicately leaving room for the vulgar or bitchy interpretation to be made, should the listener so desire. This fragile and subtle creation is cheapened if the receiver of gossip lacks sensitivity and crudely spells it out.

'They were dressed and pointing up at the ceiling and sort of wobbling in time to the music.'

'The Jarretts?' asked the publican.

'No, their backsides.'

'It sounds pretty innocuous to me. I should think that most people in this pub do some pretty strange things with their spouses when they think they are in private.'

'I know they do,' said Lindy. This caused a thoughtful silence. Lindy, as district nurse, was an unexploded minefield of gossip. Through her job, she had learned just about everything about everyone for miles around and had a habit of staring at you with an enigmatic smile playing at the corner of her lips. It could be highly disconcerting and was the only known device for halting Kelvin in full conversational flow.

Consequently there was silence until the commander came through the door. 'There are strange things going on at the bottom of the village,' he said, as he eased himself on to a stool. 'Some American lady in the Jarretts' house yelled at me to throw my shoulders back and lift my chin as I went past. She sounded just like the drill instructor at Dartmouth. It gave me a very nasty turn.'

It was duly noted that their house in River Lane was worth keeping an eye on, but no pub-frequenting villager could dream up a good enough excuse to get inside to find out what was happening. This was rectified a few weeks later when a notice appeared on the board in the post office announcing that the local branch of the SDP was being set up, with its inaugural meeting to be held at the Jarretts' when an election of officers would take place. Dick Hunniford and Ivor both went along as the respective chairmen of the Liberals and

Tories, as did Lindy who rather fancied Dr Owen. She had had a *penchant* for comely medics ever since her days as a student nurse.

Dick was the one who managed to sort out the problem of the loud American. He had been quietly driven into a corner by the fixed smile and determined brightness of Emily Jarrett who had wanted to know in what way Dick thought that Liberal policies differed from those of the SDP. Dick could not have told her the difference between Liberal policies and those of the Tories, so the conversation had been frustrating for both parties. However, he did manage to catch a glimpse of the Jarrett music centre while his eyes were casting around for a way out and, there on top of it, was the sleeve of a record.

'It had a picture of a lady grinning like a monkey on the front. She had a funny pointed backside and was wearing only a striped vest and long black stockings. It was called "Jane Fondle's Work Record" and she was upside down with her legs in the air. I reckon they were doing exercises like that when Jimmy looked through their window.'

With that problem safely pigeon-holed, the Jarretts seemed to take a higher profile. They donned his'n'hers tracksuits and ran about the streets of the village at odd hours of the day and night, frequently giving the older inhabitants nasty shocks when they erupted round the corner of a house, their trainer-clad feet pounding the tarmac with an assortment of village curs snapping at their heels. They would flash past, leaving nothing but the impression of their bright smiles shimmering in the air behind them and, perhaps, a few drops of sweat flicked into the faces of their beholders.

Nobody quite knew what to make of this until Frank Mattock came across them trotting up the road one day and managed to flag them down. They did not actually have much option since the lane was choked by his herd of dairy cows, undulating at a snail's pace towards the milking parlour, and there was no way of getting through them.

Frank's herd had achieved a certain notoriety when, the previous summer, it had encountered coming in the opposite direction many thousands of pounds' worth of customized white Porsche containing our local tycoon, Ross. Ross had sensibly stopped in the narrow lane to allow the cows to pass but had, less sensibly, brayed his horn when the tight fit led to some of them having to brush against his paintwork. The cows had panicked, with appalling consequences.

Cows, contrary to popular belief, are extremely emotional animals and they display their emotions by becoming loose in the bowel. The toot of Ross's horn literally scared them shitless. It was Ross's misfortune that the customizing of his motorcar had included turning it into a convertible and, by the time that the herd had passed and the car again came into view, neither Ross, nor his wife, nor the car were white any longer and all three were steaming gently in the still air.

The Jarretts were forced to slow to a walk beside Frank.

'Evening,' he said.

'Evening,' replied the Jarretts.

Frank looked at them curiously. They did not seem to be out of breath. 'Nice evening,' he added.

'Isn't it?' answered the Jarretts, smiling happily. The village knew what they did in their spare time but nobody knew why they did it. Nobody could think of any good reason why they should spend so much time running about and jumping up and down. Bill thought that the most likely explanation was that it had something to do with their religion. The communards, who seemed to change their religion rather more often than they probably changed their underwear, had made us aware of such matters. However, Frank thought he would try to get to the bottom of their motivation.

'Nice evening for a walk,' he said.

'We were jogging, actually,' replied Emily.

'Jogging? Is that what it's called?' Frank savoured the word. 'Jogging. And why would you be jogging?'

'For exercise.'

'For exercise?' Frank was a windsucker, blessed with a local characteristic. Its exponents tended to repeat what was being said to them and then drew air sharply in through their pursed lips with an audible sucking sound. In spite of his *penchant* for gold rings, bracelets and displaying his hairy chest, Frank was still very much a ponderous, careful-thinking countryman. 'And why would you be wanting to take exercise?' No countryman takes exercise for its own sake or even considers it: it comes as a by-product of the way of life.

'I exercise so that I am comfortable in my body,' replied Emily.

Frank continued to plod along after the swaying rumps of his cows, his stick driving holes in the verge where the grass took over from the tarmac.

'I don't quite understand that,' he said, after a bit of thought.

'What?'

'How exercise can make you more comfortable in your body. I mean, I can see your body and, if Mr Jarrett doesn't mind me saying so, it looks very nice —'

'No, I don't mind at all,' said Malcolm Jarrett.

'— But whether you're comfortable or not depends on whether you're sitting on a hard tractor seat or a tin-tack. So comfort is something that happens outside it, not in it.'

'That's not what I meant,' said Emily. 'You see, my body has to be listened to and strengthened.'

Frank looked sideways at Emily rather ruminatively. In the village, we were beginning to get used to this sort of conversation. The communards always managed to turn a remark as mundane as a comment on the weather into a major obscurantist philosophical discussion.

'The only time I am able to listen to my body is when my belly rumbles,' said Frank, 'or when I fart.'

'You obviously don't understand.'

'S'right,' agreed Frank.

'These days, we need to be on top of our bodies so that we can lead the intense multi-faceted lives that we demand with greater clarity and balance.'

Frank picked a grass stalk out of the hedgerow and chewed at it. He had nothing to do other than to walk along behind his cows, so he thought he might as well continue the conversation. 'It's a sort of religion, is it? All this rushing about and listening to your body.'

'No, certainly not. We have a right and a duty to be physically fit.'

'I always reckoned that staying healthy was a matter of luck.'

'Not at all. Anyone can control their own health and the length of their life. It's a matter of diet and maintaining a positive attitude,' replied Malcolm Jarrett.

'Is that right?' asked Frank.

They continued to follow the cows. Frank swished idly at the cow parsley in the hedgerow while the Jarretts skipped up and down so that they wouldn't stiffen up. It was like taking a couple of dogs for a walk, Frank reported later. They were dancing all round him, covering a dozen yards to every one of his. Still, Emily was wearing a white tracksuit and her bum was undeniably nicer to look at than those of the cows.

The Jarretts' profile continued to be high. They organized evenings of classical record music at home, although Winnie was the only regular attender. Jimmy and the Grabber turned up once just to see if there were any free drinks going, but there weren't. They achieved a certain notoriety by writing letters to the local paper condemning hunting after their motorbike, returning home from work, had been forced to stop at a road junction to allow sixty horsemen, thirty-eight motorcycle followers, 132 cars, and a woman on foot carrying a baby, to cross in front of them, all baying for blood in pursuit of an extremely knackered stag.

Most swallows went through a period when they were vociferously opposed to hunting, although not many went as far as writing rude letters to the papers about it. Hunting was such an imporant part of life in the area that it was difficult to avoid it. However, it was an unfortunate fact, that most came to realize, that the large numbers of deer in the vicinity would have been wiped out by the farmers for their depredations on crops had it not been for the love of hunting that the farmers had, bred deep in their bones over the centuries of indulgence in the sport.

It was difficult to deny that there was something distinctly odd about people who spent so much money and received so much pleasure from chasing and killing such splendid animals, but the deer probably had a better deal than the cattle who ended up in the inevitable ignominy of the slaughterhouse. The deer, at least, had a chance of living in freedom to a ripe old age and, if they met their end through a huntsman's bullet after the hounds had brought them to bay, that death was a celebration rather than mere routine.

The Jarretts' newspaper correspondence was regarded indulgently by the locals. Anti-hunting was a stage that many newcomers had to go through and it was hoped that, when they had grown out of it, they would take their natural place at the bottom of the social pyramid from where they could slowly ascend as the passing of the years turned them into figures of some significance in the community – provided they stayed long enough. It would never be possible for them to reach the eminence of people like Kelvin and Jimmy who had actually been born in the village, but others like Ivor and Lindy had risen remarkably quickly. Lindy was regarded as an equal by most of the locals and she had lived in the area for only fifteen years, while the dazzling example of the commander, who had managed to get on the committee of the horticultural society within five years of moving to the village, was an inspiration to all swallows and a solid refutation of the charge that the locals were inclined to be hostile to newcomers.

However, it took time for incomers to learn their place in society and, during that first year or two, their social judgement tended to be poor. The Jarretts soon went above their station in life again. In the late autumn, another notice appeared on the board in the post office. 'Challenge', it was headed, followed by 'The Social Democratic Party challenges the Liberal and Conservative Parties to a Grand Quiz'.

Ivor and Dick and their committees went into a huddle to agree a mutual strategy. They concluded that, although it would probably be wiser to ignore these social and political upstarts, it was just within the dignity of their respective parties to approach the issuers of the challenge and find out what they had in mind. It was devastatingly simple. There would be a panel of three people to represent each party. A quizmaster was to be found who would be mutually acceptable and members of the public would be charged an admission fee of 50p. The winning team would take the kitty to add to party funds.

It was felt that the challenge could not be ignored, although there were obvious difficulties. The Jarretts were both teachers and therefore must be awesomely bright. They listened to classical music and took both the *Observer* and the *Sunday Times* at the weekend. Who would be the questionmaster? This was a really knotty one which nearly caused the whole idea to founder. In the end, it was decided that the quiz would be divided into three parts, each section presided over by a different questioner to be nominated by each party. It was further agreed that there should be no prior collusion between the team and its questionmaster and that there should be a ten-minute break between each section to allow drinks to be replenished. The venue was to be the church hall and the date the week before Christmas. A book was opened in the pub: the SDP evens, Tories 2 to 1 against and Liberals 3 to 1. The excitement was intense.

Chapter Eleven

THE CHURCH HALL was normally used only once a month for meetings of the parochial church council. It had once been used for parish council meetings, but its members had passed a unanimous vote just before the war which changed their venue to a room in the pub. This was a great aid to the free exchange of ideas and had considerably increased the quantity, if not the quality, of the oratory. The hall itself was a dank, miserable room used primarily for the storage of trestle tables and chairs that had last seen the light of day at the jubilee of King George V. It also had a pile of old saucepans in one corner which a previous vicar had collected with the intention of transforming them into a Spitfire, but the war had ended before a sufficient quantity had accumulated to make it worthwhile for them to be pressed into service.

There were two items on the walls that could be considered decorative. On one side of the room hung a splendid Georgian wall clock and, opposite, was a large print entitled *The Light of the World*, with the figure of Christ holding up his lamp, looking as if he were trying to peer through the fly spots that dotted the picture-glass to read the time on the clock.

There was always a thick layer of dust over everything. The caretaker, whose responsibility it was to keep the place clean, was also clock winder and organist at the church, but he had been corrupted by his part-time assistant, the Grabber.

The latter kept an eye out for coach parties arriving in the village. When they appeared he would rush up to the caretaker's cottage from where they would both repair to the church. As the tourists entered the church, the high spot of any tour of the village, they would be greeted by the caretaker playing tunes on the organ like *Bless this House* and *Danny Boy* with every ounce of pathos that he could deliver and, just as they were about to reach for their hankies, the Grabber would emerge from the vestry, bearing a collection plate and intoning, 'Give alms to the poor of the parish.' The two of them made a fortune during the tourist season and it all passed across the bar in the pub.

By the time the contestants gathered in the pub on the evening of the contest, it had become a real needle match as the Tories had let slip that they had obtained a letter from the Sniffer MP thanking the other two parties for contributing to Conservative funds. This was to be read out in the event of their victory. Their team consisted of Dennis, the commander and Kelvin, which immediately caused their odds to lengthen to 6 to 1 against during a flurry of late-struck bargains. The SDP had the Jarretts and Winnie, their only other paid-up member, while the Liberals had Dick Hunniford, Mary Mowbray and Lindy.

Business in the pub boomed. In fact, the evening became a testimony to the amount that the local citizenry could drink, once they put their minds to it. Most of the contestants were already there loosening up their brain cells, while the

spectators were stoking up for a long evening ahead. The Jarretts had obviously given up training for the day and were downing large quantities of whisky, which was an encouraging sign that they might be preparing to participate properly in this, the most important cultural activity of the community. They and the rest of the protagonists were standing to one side of the bar trying to look blasé and important while the future audience examined them to try to pick up hints as to their future form.

Mary Mowbray came in through the pub door and fought her way to the bar. Her ruddy complexion was highlighted by a large piece of white sticking plaster across her forehead.

'What happened to you, Mary?' asked the commander.

'I walked into a door,' she replied grimly.

'What a shame! Can I buy you a drink?'

'Just an orange juice, please. The doctor told me to lay off for a few days.'

'That's dreadful. If I were you, I'd change my doctor.'

The commander handed her an orange juice and she looked round the raucously crowded pub. 'Where's Dennis? I've got a bone to pick with him.'

'He should be along any minute,' answered Ivor. 'What's he done?'

'Never you mind. Ah! Here he comes now.'

Dennis elbowed his way up to the bar. 'What ho, chaps!' he said. 'Ready for the fray?' Dennis sometimes used expressions that were rather old-fashioned. He had once called a tourist whom he had nearly run down 'old bean', which had been construed as a deadly insult and had brought out a volley of abuse. He saw Mary and her plaster. 'Mary! What on earth has happened to you? Grenville did not mention anything about it last night. They must be dangerous, those WI meetings.'

'I thought it must have been you,' said Mary. 'Who else came out last night?'

'Frank Mattock was along. Why? What's this about?'

'You should be ashamed of yourself! It's all your fault that I've hurt my head.'

Dennis looked a bit bewildered. 'I don't quite understand.

All we did was have a few drinks and help Grenville pluck your chickens because you were at your meeting.'

'A few drinks! Grenville was in a drunken stupor – it was quite disgraceful. And as for that trick you played, it was quite disgusting! And damned irresponsible.'

'Oh, you saw that did you?'

'I did.'

'What's all this about?' asked the commander.

Dennis looked a bit embarrassed. 'Well, you know, we had a few drinks and plucked and gutted a few chickens and had a few more drinks and Grenville fell asleep in front of the Aga. It was all very harmless.'

'That doesn't sound that awful,' said the commander.

'And what about that chicken neck?' demanded Mary. 'I suppose that was your idea?'

'Oh no. That was Frank's.'

'What about a chicken neck?' prompted the commander.

'Well, Frank had this idea for a joke, you see. Grenville was asleep and just before we went he put this chicken neck so that it was poking out of Grenville's trousers. It looked jolly realistic. We thought it might give him a bit of a fright when he woke up.' There was a guffaw of laughter from round the bar.

'That's not so bad, Mary,' said the commander. 'Where's your sense of humour?'

'I left it in the doctor's surgery,' replied Mary. 'When I got home, I went into the kitchen and there was Grenville, still sound asleep, and there was the neck. I could have handled that all right, but when I went in the dog was sitting in front of my dear husband chewing it and when I screamed, it pulled it out. I fainted and cracked my head on the Aga. And don't anyone dare laugh.'

'Heavens!' said Dennis, spluttering a bit. 'How absolutely appalling for you. I'm most dreadfully sorry. We should have thought of that and shut the dog out of the kitchen. It is a cocker spaniel after all. And what's its name again?'

'Willy,' said the commander.

One we had wiped the orange juice off the commander and Dennis, the pub emptied as we repaired across the road to the church hall. It had been transformed for the occasion. Two paraffin heaters had been working for most of the day and the chill had been driven back to the corners of the room. It had been dusted down and Winnie had arranged vases of flowers on the four tables – one for each team and one for the questionmasters – which had been erected in front of sixty or so chairs. There was an expectant hum of conversation as people settled themselves in partisan groups.

The vicar was quizmaster for the SDP, the squire for the Tories and the Liberals had chosen Muriel, which had annoyed her sister Barbara, both because she had not been selected and because Muriel had no business in supporting the Liberals. The questioners went into a huddle to establish the order of play and the vicar was selected to open the bowling.

It immediately became clear why the SDP had chosen him. His opening question brought dismayed looks from the Liberals and Tories and a buzz of consternation ran round all those who had put money on the two outsiders.

'Who was the son of Jephunneh?'

Who indeed? Who or perhaps even *what* is or was Jephunneh? The question was rapidly passed down the line of Tories and Liberals to the SDP and Emily Jarrett looked expectantly at Winnie. With the cat-at-the-cream look adopted by every smart Alec on every TV quiz show, she trotted out, 'Joshua the son of Nun, and Caleb the son of Jephunneh, were the only two, who ever got through, to the land of milk and honey.'

'Ting' went Ivor on his little bell and the SDP received bonus marks, putting them five points in the lead. The Tories and Liberals swallowed nervous gulps of their drinks to bolster their confidence, while the SDP celebrated with whisky and a discreet sip of sherry for Winnie. The publican had taken the precaution of establishing a team of runners at the door and there was no danger that the contestants might be stricken by drought.

Winnie's father had been a Methodist lay preacher and the first dozen questions were aimed mercilessly at her sphere of knowledge: who was Zelophehad?; name eight of the tribes of Israel; how old was Methuselah when he finally shuffled off his mortal coil? The Liberals were nowhere and the Tories were only saved from a whitewash when Dennis managed to dredge the names of the three who were stuffed into the fiery furnace from the depths of his subconscious mind and elicited the first round of applause of the evening from all those who had backed his team at 6 to 1.

The vicar's second round was literature. The Jarretts answered all their questions and scavenged hungrily for bonus points among the wreckage of the answers hesitantly submitted by the other teams. Dennis again saved the Tories by displaying an unexpected knowledge of the works of Charles Dickens and Lindy managed to break the Liberal duck by knowing that the Jabberwock was slain by a vorpal sword. The vicar's third and final round of questions was more even. He had chosen to concentrate on science and technology and none of the contestants was able to differentiate between a byte and a ram, Cobol or Basic, or was capable of hazarding an intelligent guess as to what the letters of the word laser might stand for. Lindy scored the only points when he strayed into biology, while both Jarretts were overruled by Ivor when they tried to dispute the length of time required to burn up the calories in an ounce of butter if one was playing squash.

The vicar's incumbency of the chair ended with the SDP scoring sixty-five points, the Tories fifteen and the Liberals ten. The ten-minute break was a desperate business. Bill closed the book on the SDP and he could find nobody prepared to back either of the other teams. Even Dick Hunniford refused to back himself at 33 to 1. The pub was packed as the interval stretched to twenty minutes and the unfortunate Mary Mowbray was the only member of either team who was still entirely sober by the time that the bell tinged to announce the squire's term of office. His first question was to the SDP.

'Who saw him die?'

'I beg your pardon?' asked Malcolm Jarrett, the team captain.

'Who saw him die?' repeated the squire.

The team went into a huddle. 'We don't quite understand the question,' said the captain.

The squire reddened a bit. 'It's a perfectly simple question. Who saw him die?'

'Who saw who die?'

'Don't be so damn silly. If I told you who saw who die, then I'd be giving you the answer. That's your job. Mine's to do the asking.'

'But there isn't enough information in the question to give a sensible answer. There could be hundreds of answers. Hardy saw Nelson die, for example.'

'Wrong. I offer it for a bonus.'

'Mr Umpire, I would like to enter a protest.'

The audience was enjoying this. It was not much fun watching other people showing off, but it was lovely when they could not get the answers and began to lose their cool.

'Overruled,' said Ivor. 'The answer's obviously "the fly". It's from *Cock Robin*, isn't it, squire? "I, said the fly, with my little eye." '

'Quite right, Ivor. Next question —'

'The fly,' said Kelvin.

The squire paused. 'What are you talking about?'

'You offered it for a bonus and the answer's "the fly".'

'But the correct answer's already been given.'

'Ah yes, but Ivor's not playing. He's just the umpire. I'm the first contestant to give it.'

'Don't be absurd,' said the squire.

'Actually, I think Kelvin's right,' said Ivor. 'You did offer it for a bonus and it was wrong of me to answer. Did you know what the right answer was before I gave it, Kelvin?'

'Yes,' replied Kelvin stoutly.

'In that case, I award you a bonus point.'

'I protest,' said Malcolm Jarrett.

'So do I,' said Dick. 'Anyone could have said "the fly".'

'But Kelvin was the only person who did. Anyway, that's the first question he has answered and how many others do you think he's going to get right?'

The other contestants could hardly argue with that and as the audience thought that Kelvin deserved his point as well, the squire moved on. 'Mrs Jarrett, what have cow, horse and goat got in common?'

There was another SDP huddle. 'They are all grass-eating quadrupeds which could well be ruminants and they can be seen in the British countryside. They're all domesticated mammals . . . Is that enough?'

'No. I offer it —'

'Hang on,' said Emily, 'we haven't finished yet . . . er . . . they can all be found within the parish. They can all be eaten . . . er . . .'

'Ting' went Ivor. 'Your time is up. I offer it for a bonus.'

'The second letter of each word is "o",' said Mary.

'Right,' said the squire.

'That's ridiculous,' said Malcolm indignantly.

'If you abuse the questionmaster, you'll have points deducted,' warned Ivor.

Malcolm, the unaccustomed whisky coursing through his veins, opened his mouth to say more in spite of some hissing from all those spectators who were backing the other teams, but Emily obviously and painfully kicked him on the ankle and he shut up.

'Next question,' said the squire. 'When did mains electricity come to the village?'

'1959,' said Dick promptly.

Malcolm avoided his wife's foot and spoke up again. 'How could we be expected to know that?'

'How could we be expected to know all that stuff about books that the vicar asked?' said Dick.

'That's common knowledge to everyone who's well-read.'

'The electricity is common knowledge to everyone who lives round here.'

'Nonsense,' said Malcolm belligerently.

The squire was getting cross. 'If there's one thing I hate, it's someone who belly-aches. Kindly control yourself.'

'Piss off,' said Malcolm.

Ivor tinged his bell. 'Any further unwarranted interruptions or abuse will result in the deduction of points,' he warned.

Malcolm glared, but held his peace.

The squire cleared his throat. 'What are the colours of the old Etonian tie?'

'Light and dark blue,' answered Dennis.

'And the colours of a Guards tie, Mr Jarrett?'

'Blue, with a British Rail symbol on it.'

'I meant the Brigade of Guards – the army brigade.'

Malcolm muttered, 'Ridiculous old fascist,' under his breath but refused to try a guess.

'Dark red and dark blue,' said Dennis.

'Well done, Dennis. You're doing jolly well,' said the squire approvingly. 'Dick, how many rows of pews are there in the church?'

Dick looked blank.

'Eighteen,' yelled the Grabber from the audience.

'Eighteen,' said Dick.

'Quite correct.'

Ivor frowned at the spectators. 'I must ask the audience to keep quiet.'

'Mary,' said the squire, 'who commanded the first British unit into Brussels during the last war?'

'How on earth am I supposed to know that?' she asked.

Malcolm smirked rather drunkenly.

'It's an important part of military history,' said the squire.

'Well, I've no idea. Montgomery?'

'No, I offer it for a bonus.' There was silence. 'I did.'

'You did what?' asked Mary.

'I commanded the first British unit into Brussels.'

Mandyandkeith in the audience began to clap, but nobody else joined in. The squire looked a bit disappointed.

The squire's round brought the Tories up to within twenty points of the SDP, but the odds that Bill was offering on the Liberals in the pub during the interval were now 50 to 1. Muriel managed to change all that, however. Instead of the bits of paper that the others had fumbled through in order to ask their questions, she was equipped with a tray covered in a lacy tablecloth. When Ivor tinged to announce the opening the session, she whisked off the cloth.

'I couldn't think of any questions and so we shall have a memory test. On this tray are forty-five everyday objects. Each team can examine it for one minute and then they have five minutes to list as many of those objects as they can remember.'

The Liberals won, of course, taking home £22.50, less the cost of the tea and biscuits that were on offer at the end of the evening. Mary Mowbray was the only person on either team who was sufficiently sober by Muriel's round to remember more than half a dozen of the objects. She managed thirty, while Dennis and Malcolm Jarrett were so appalled by the task confronting them that they both fell asleep before the end of their five minutes. The real winners were the publican, who had one of the best evenings of the year, and Muriel. She had placed a £3 bet at 50 to 1 and soaked up all the profits that Bill had been counting on. She donated £5 of it to party funds.

Chapter Twelve

THE COMMANDER had had a bad week. His pig had escaped only a few days before it was due to be hacked into small pieces and hung up in the chimney to smoke. The beast had found his cauliflowers and had rampaged up and down their neatly regimented rows before breaking into a shed and eating a packet of weed killer. He was now gloomily waiting for it to die. That was not all. He had sold some eggs to the hotel, one of which had contained an almost fully developed chick that had sent the chef, an ex-debutante graduate of a Cordon Bleu cookery course, into hysterics and quite ruined a batch of meringues.

The commander had been coming into the pub in an ill temper all week and his mood had grown increasingly foul as he poured the barley wines down his throat.

'It's a backwater, this place. Nothing but a backwater. Nothing has changed and nothing has happened for centuries. I sometimes wonder what the hell I'm doing here.'

'Making a living?' proffered Dennis cautiously.

'Making a living! That's a joke for a start. I could have gone into industry or into the City when I left the navy. Man management: that's what I'm qualified for. I could take men half-way round the world and they were willing to fight and die when they got there.'

'Pigs are different, though,' said Kelvin. 'Pigs aren't as easy to handle as people. They don't know what's good for them.'

The commander brooded for a bit. 'My brain is turning to porridge. You can't help turning into a country bumpkin out here. There's no stimulation. What is there to talk about? Tell me that?'

'Money, sex, politics, religion, sport, human nature, current affairs, literature, art,' said Lindy. 'It's very restrictive.'

'I know. It's dreadful. This area is a cultural desert. There isn't a theatre for miles.'

Malcolm Jarrett, our local intellectual, had been holding his peace until now, but felt he could contribute here. 'There's nothing to stop you going up to Stratford.'

'Ah,' said the commander. 'If only I could afford it. But it's so far away and it would just cost too much to get there.'

'I suppose you couldn't spare the time, either.'

'It's not so much that. After all, the cabbages will keep on growing whether I'm there to watch them or not. It's just that I can't justify the cost.'

'Aye. That's the trouble, it's the expense,' agreed Kelvin.

That was the attitude which made the usual scruffy assortment of characters round the bar, nursing their glasses of beer, worth about ten times their urban counterparts. They were willing to spend any amount of money on their businesses, but virtually nothing on their leisure, pleasure or what might make their lives or those of their families more comfortable.

'Yes,' said Dennis, getting into the spirit of things. 'If only I could afford to go, I would love it.'

'That's easy enough to arrange,' said Malcolm. 'We've got an "A" level class going up from the college next week and there'll be plenty of spare seats on the bus. You could all come if you wanted.'

There was a short silence. Malcolm looked enquiringly at the commander. 'Oh,' he said, 'I'm rather busy next week. What day is it going up?'

'What days can't you manage?' asked Malcolm cruelly.

'Let's think,' said the commander, a bit embarrassed about finding himself on the spot. 'Well, Thursday's market day. Couldn't do that.'

'No, couldn't do Thursday,' echoed Kelvin.

'If that bloody pig survives, I'm hoping to take it to the abattoir on Tuesday, and on Friday I've got the VAT man coming round. What day is the bus going up?'

'I think it's Wednesday.'

'What a shame! That's when I have to get stuff ready to take to market.'

'Isn't it a pity,' said Dennis. 'I would have loved to go up as well. If only it had been Monday.'

'Yes,' chorused half those in the pub. 'If only it had been Monday.'

'I'd've liked a nice bit of Shakespeare,' said Kelvin, who sounded as if he equated it with a nice bit of pork. 'Monday would be my only free day.'

Malcolm Jarrett had got it wrong, of course. It had been Monday all along and he was wise enough in the ways of the village to contact all those who had expressed an interest by telephone to prevent any further collusion on excuses. There were some rather glum meetings in the street and in the post office where it was discovered just who was in for a large dose of culture.

The commander was going, as were Kelvin, myself, Lindy, Dennis, Mary Mowbray and an ancient couple who were cousins of some kind to Kelvin. It was never safe to inquire too closely into relationships between 'cousins' or even nieces and nephews. It all too often uncovered details that would have caused instant combustion to the relevant page of the Book of Common Prayer.

We all met outside the post office at 7.30 am, late enough to allow the morning agricultural chores to have been completed. We were not a particularly happy bunch. It was late October; it was still fairly dark and there was frost on the ground. Most of us were muffled in coats or padded jackets, but Kelvin was wearing his smart suit with a thick woolly pullover beneath. We had to go into town to meet the bus and so we all piled into the commander's estate car – one of those foreign eight-seater jobs – which he used to transport courgettes and mushrooms to market and bring back piles of rotting horse manure to give the aforesaid mushrooms something to feed on.

Town was half an hour away, but it was only fifteen minutes before Kelvin's cousins began to fall apart. This was a phenomenon I had heard about, but never witnessed. The village had housed a famous old lady who had died ten years earlier at the age of ninety-five. In all her years, she had never been more than 1½ miles from the house in which she had been born; she had never seen the sea, which was only 10 miles away across the moor. Kelvin's cousins were out of the same mould. They had been to town before, but now they were faced by a four-hour journey up the motorway to Stratford. They had been able to come to terms with the idea in abstract, but the reality proved too much for them. They were gentle old people, so there was nothing loud or raucous about their funny turns. The old woman, who had been introduced as Mercy, leaned politely over the back of her seat and was sick over Kelvin's going-to-the-theatre trousers.

Kelvin had been contemplating the slowly lightening morning with a certain foreboding himself, but Mercy's action brought his attention back to current matters. 'You daft old biddy,' he yelled.

The commander had been having his difficulties as well. He had been quietly swearing to himself about the instability of his car due to the abnormal weight of his seven passengers, but the sudden sensory shocks brought about by the violent assault of Kelvin's yell on his eardrums and on his olfactory nerves by Mercy's regurgitation of her breakfast Rice Krispies made him swerve violently across the bows of one of the many milk tankers that ply the country lanes in the early morning. He pulled up by the hedge.

The doors of the car were flung open and, before the wondering gaze of the tanker driver who had been forced to stop, we all jumped out of the vehicle. The commander seemed to have lost his cool completely, which made one feel thankful on behalf of those matelots whom he expected to fight and die for him that his nerve had never been put to the test under fire. He was standing in the middle of the road, wringing his hands.

'My car, my poor car. It'll never be the same again. It'll stink for as long as I own it.'

Kelvin's cousins were standing on the verge, he with his arm round her, looking like a pair of elderly dormice. 'Mercy's very sorry. But her nerves got the better of her.'

'What can I do? What can I do?' moaned the commander.

Lindy went over to check on Mercy and then peered into the car at Kelvin. After his initial outburst, he appeared to be in a state of shock. The tanker driver switched on his hazard warning lights and climbed down from his cab.

'What the hell's going on?' he asked. 'Oh, hullo, Dennis.'

Before he had decided that he did not like work, Dennis had been one of the farmers from whom the driver had collected milk. Farmers all tried to remain on excellent terms with their tanker drivers because it was they who decided how much milk was actually picked up each day and thus had considerable influence on their incomes. At Christmas, milk lorries groaned under the weight of gift bottles of whisky and gin.

'Good morning, Vic,' replied Dennis. 'One of our passengers has been sick.'

'All over the interior of my car,' moaned the commander.

Some strangled grunts brought it to our notice that Kelvin was coming round. They developed into an indignant squawk. 'It's not your bloody car that's suffered, it's my trousers!' he shouted as he bent himself into contortions extricating himself from the dicky seat of the car.

'Really?' said the commander, perking up a bit. He pushed Kelvin out of the way so that he could see into the car. 'Oh, wonderful! It seems to be all right. Your trousers seem to have taken it all. Isn't that a relief?'

'Now we've got that cleared up, hadn't we better be getting on our way?' said Lindy. 'Otherwise we'll miss the bus.'

'I think Mercy and I would be better off going home,' said Kelvin's cousin.

'And if you think I'm going to spend the rest of the day in these trousers, you're wrong,' said Kelvin, who was gingerly trying to hold them away from his legs. 'I'm going home to change.'

'But we'll miss the bus,' said the commander.

'What's all this about?' asked the driver. He was waving cars past his lorry.

'We're all supposed to be meeting a bus in town but Kelvin wants to go home to change his trousers and those two just want to go home. If we take them back, we'll miss the bus,' said Ivor.

'That's no problem. The three of them can squeeze into the cab with me. I'm on my way up to the village.'

'But how will I get back in time for the bus?' asked Kelvin.

'You won't.'

'That's not fair,' he said, reverting to childhood.

Vic had the solution. 'I know. Why don't you change trousers with the old man? You're much the same size.' Both Kelvin and the old man looked horrified. The idea of exposing any of their flesh or their undergarments in public was too awful to contemplate. They belonged to the old school and were reluctant even to roll up their shirt sleeves on a sunny day.

'His trousers won't match my jacket,' said Kelvin.

Lindy, used to dealing with such people, understood their difficulty. 'That won't matter, Kelvin. I suggest that all the men form a circle round you. Like they do at rugby internationals when someone loses their shorts.'

Kelvin, with his back to the wall, was capable of rising to the occasion. 'I'm not stripping off in the middle of the road. What I'm going to do is change in the cab of the lorry.' He climbed up to unveil himself and the rest of us moved over to the old man to persuade him to do the same.

Then a police car arrived. The situation could have been better. The road at this point was too narrow to merit a white line to define the centre and the commander's car and the milk tanker were causing a considerable impediment to the free flow of traffic. Not that there was much traffic, but that was not the point. The policeman pulled up behind the lorry and came up to tap on the window of the cab.

Kelvin, had he had any sense, would have wound down the window and explained that he was a retired special constable, a man of great integrity and probity who was in the process of examining his longjohns to see whether they, too, needed to be changed. It seemed, though, that he looked briefly up and said, 'Get knotted.'

The policeman had rather a short fuse and he began to beat on the cab door. Kelvin, somewhat alarmed by this display, locked it. We became aware of the disturbance and moved round from the front of the lorry to see what was going on.

'What the hell do you think you're playing at, hitting my door like that?' asked the driver.

'So it's your door, is it?' said the policeman. The sort of policemen that we knew travelled around in Land Rovers or rusty Ford Escorts and were given short shrift if they tried to 'come the copper' on us. This particular one seemed to be rather far from his native habitat. He was wearing an orange jacket and his vehicle was one of those large saloons that are normally to be seen sliding down the fast lane of motorways, all flashing lights and dayglo paint, with the back seat piled high with traffic cones.

'I've just said so, you daft pillock. Look,' Vic said, pointing at his overall, 'it says "Milk Marketing Board" on my pocket and it says "Milk Marketing Board" on the lorry.'

The policeman strode over to Vic and loomed at him, menacingly. 'Who are you calling a daft pillock?'

'Who was it who was thumping on the door of my lorry? You could have damaged it.'

'*If* it's your lorry. What's that bloke doing in the cab, then?'

'He's taking off his trousers.'

That rocked the policeman a bit, but he was not about to let it interfere with his duty. 'Whatever he's up to, get this road cleared or else I'll book you for obstruction.' He would have been inhuman had he left matters there, however. 'Why's he taking off his trousers anyway?'

'Because she was sick on them.'

The policeman turned to inspect the guilty 'she'. Mercy, who was behind the commander's car, was tugging at her husband's boots as he lay on the ground.

'What's she doing?'

'What does it look like? She's trying to get his boots off.'

'Why's she taking off his boots?'

'So that he can get his trousers off.'

The policeman looked suspiciously at Vic. 'Are you taking the mickey?'

'No.'

'OK, then, why does that one want to get his trousers off?'

'So that the one in the cab taking his trousers off can go to Stratford to see Shakespeare.'

The policeman thought for a bit. These town bobbies, as this one surely was, have to learn that the rural brain works rather differently from the urban brain. The city villain is always looking for ways to go round the law so that he can commit an offence that he knows is naughty. The rural villain constantly finds the law putting itself between him and something that he considers perfectly all right – such as poaching – or else niggling away at the outcroppings of bureaucracy in the case of tractor licences and checking that the pub stops serving drinks at closing time. The police tend to be looked at as interfering busy-bodies rather than menacing figures of authority.

'You'll have to come up with a better story than that. He can't be going to see Shakespeare. He's been dead for years.'

Satisfying this guardian of the law was a very complicated business, but eventually we passed the old man's trousers through the lorry window to Kelvin. Dennis, grumbling at the sacrilege, gave up a couple of sheets of his *Times* to fabricate a kilt for the de-trousered one to appease the policeman's sense of decency. The boy in blue then led us, carving through the non-existent traffic with his light flashing, and we made the bus with minutes to spare.

The trip up was very peaceful. The students were provincial punk, daringly stretching to a stud in one ear, and many of them were nice, clean-living members of the Young Farmers' Club. They sat in the back of the coach where they giggled, played mini-computer games and listened to Abba on their personal stereos. We were under the control of Martha, a lecturer in the English department of the college. Dennis fell asleep. The commander and Kelvin looked out of the window and marvelled at all the rich farmland we were passing, and Mary lectured Martha on the finer points of dressage.

By the time we reached Stratford, we had found out that the play was *Julius Caesar*, that we had to pay for our seats since the munificence of the education authority only went as far as the bus, and that Kelvin had a deep passion for the actress playing Portia, having had her imprinted on his brain as she was the first moving object that he had ever seen on television when he had finally decided to buy one – 26-inch colour with a built-in cocktail cabinet – six years earlier.

The students vanished as soon as they disembarked from the bus while the adults stood round in an uncertain circle, wondering just how to occupy themselves until the play started at 7.30. It dawned on me that we were tourists, part of that despised under-race that clogged the streets of the village during the summer months. The commander was the only one of us who had ever had experience of being one of this breed in the past and his tourism had taken place in the gut of Valetta, the reeking opium dens of Macao and possibly even a gracious bordello or two in New Orleans. He was not much good at the home-grown variety. He and Dennis moved across the road from the bus station and gazed with horror into a shop window filled with dolls dressed as beefeaters, Anne Hathaways and all the members of the royal family.

'Right,' said Martha. 'What does everyone want to do?'

'I came here to go to the theatre,' said Kelvin.

'Yes, we all did. But the play doesn't start for seven hours.'

'We could have left later, then, and I wouldn't have had that awful rush to feed the stock this morning.'

'You mean for Prudence to feed the stock while you drank your tea,' said Dennis.

'Bloody cheek!' said Kelvin.

Martha clapped her hands together. 'Come on, now. Pay attention.' She had realized that the group she was with would be as difficult to control as any of her students. 'What I would suggest is that we all have lunch together and then go and see some of the sights.'

We strolled up the street, casting indifferent eyes over half-timbered Tudor buildings and making disparaging comments about the displayed menus and the ugliness of the passers-by as opposed to those back home.

'How about a Chinese meal?' suggested the commander.

'Foreign muck,' said Kelvin automatically.

'I'm told they always have English food on the menu and they're usually very cheap.'

Kelvin was overruled and we trooped suspiciously upstairs into the first-floor restaurant. Martha, fortunately, was a true child of our urban culture, which meant that she knew her way round a Chinese menu. A town of at least five thousand people is needed to support a Chinese restaurant and our village was 15 miles from such a conurbation. So the subtle

mysteries of foo yung, chow mein and chop suey were as veiled to members of our community as the cuisine of the highlands of New Guinea. There was an uneasy silence as we studied the menu.

'What's sweet-and-sour?' asked Dennis.

Martha looked up from her menu with a startled expression. 'Sweet-and-sour? You must know. Deep-fried bits of pork or whatever coated in batter in a sweet-and-sour sauce.'

'But is it nice?'

'Yes, I suppose so. It's not what I go for, personally, but it's probably the most popular Chinese dish.'

'I once spent a fortnight in Hong Kong,' said the commander. 'But I don't remember any of this sort of stuff. I had some sea-snake once and the lady I was with had a thousand-year egg, but she said it was nothing like as old as that. It had probably been laid in the past decade.'

Kelvin's alarm bells were ringing. 'You mean they serve you snakes and rotten eggs?'

'They're considered a great delicacy.'

'But an egg that old wouldn't even be rotten. It would have dried up completely.'

'I don't think it can have done. Anyway I don't suppose a rotten egg is any worse than some of the things you eat.'

'Nonsense. I eat good fresh food.'

'And you have to get Prudence to shake the maggots off the venison you poach.'

'That's different.'

'So's a thousand-year egg.'

The neatly-bottomed waiter, wearing the manic grin of his branch of the profession, appeared at the end of our table. 'Order, Sir?' he asked in an oriental approximation of a Midlands accent.

'We're not quite ready yet,' said Martha. He bowed politely and withdrew, padding down to the other end of the restaurant, past the sprinkling of businessmen insulating themselves from the embarrassment of having to catch each other's eyes behind copies of the morning papers. The waiter straightened out a napkin and glided back to our table.

'We're still not ready,' said the commander testily, trying to equate his memories of Hong Kong with the Chinglish of the menu. The waited bowed and withdrew a couple of yards to scrutinize us with infinite contempt.

'Shall I order for us all?' suggested Martha.

'That sounds like a good idea,' said Lindy.

'I want a steak and an omelette,' announced Kelvin. 'They can't muck up that.'

'All right. I'll order Chinese for the rest of us and you can be on your own.' The waiter, who had been quivering beside us like a Labrador waiting for the order to retrieve, jumped forward. 'We'd like a 67, a 32, a 43 —'

The waiter peered over her shoulder at the menu. '67, that is sliced duck and bean shoots. What is 32?'

They laboriously worked out the order.

'I never know why they bother to give the dishes numbers,' said Martha, after the waiter had retreated to a hatch and bawled the order through. 'They never know them.'

'Perhaps it's something to do with their accounts,' said Dennis. 'Ivor is a tax commissioner and he was telling me that there was a Chink up in front of them who claimed he fed his family on the leftovers from the customers' plates. He got away with it, too.'

'Well, I'll make sure I spit on anything that I leave behind,' said Kelvin. 'Just because these people are foreigners, there's no reason why they should be allowed to get away with not paying their taxes.'

It was doubtful whether Kelvin had ever paid any tax in his life. Even within the last couple of years, on the rare occasions that he put his hand into his pocket, he often pulled out one of the old white fivers. Up to five years previously, he had even been in the habit of paying with a gold sovereign, no doubt hoarded away by a tax-avoiding ancestor. That had been very popular locally until some spoil-sport of a visitor had told him in the pub that they were now worth more than fifty times the face value.

We sat and waited for our food. Martha occupied us by providing a crash course on the life and times of William Shakespeare with particular reference to Stratford and to a well-practised outline of the plot and deeper meaning of *Julius*

Caesar. The waiter returned, bringing steaming trays of food which he laid down on the table.

'It's certainly very colourful,' said Mary critically. It was certainly that: lurid reds, yellows and greens – all that was missing was blue, which has never been a wildly popular colour for food. We had oval plates while Kelvin's was round with his omelette reposing in the middle of it. He looked at it mournfully.

'Where's my steak?' he asked. The waiter had done his waiting and had gone behind the bar to pick his teeth and examine the breasts of the foreign devil on page 3. Kelvin tried to catch his eye and failed, so he summoned him as he was wont to summon his sheepdog – by sticking a couple of gnarled fingers in his mouth and emitting a whistle. The whistle was designed to catch the attention of an elderly, half-deaf canine a couple of fields away and it sliced through the chapel-like silence of the restaurant and almost knocked the waiter off his stool. There was a rustle of disapproving *Daily Telegraphs* from the other tables, which was silenced by a glare from Kelvin. Dennis and Martha looked pained.

'You can be really uncouth,' complained Dennis.

'Don't blame me. Blame that waiter for not bringing me the dinner that I asked for,' replied Kelvin.

'Lunch,' murmured Dennis as the waiter approached.

'Sah?' said the waiter. 'You whistle?'

'That's right, chum. I whistle. Where's my steak?'

The waiter looked at Kelvin's plate. 'You order omelette and there is omelette.'

'I also order steak. Isn't that right?' Kelvin appealed for support from round the table with limited success since the rest of us were fully absorbed in the engrossing task of trying to help ourselves to precisely one fifth of everything whilst trying to make the fifths closer to quarters in the case of the more interesting dishes. 'Well, I did, anyway.'

The waiter gave Kelvin a supercilious look but picked up his order book and leafed through it. 'Ah so!' he said in the best Charlie Chan manner. 'Quite ri'. You do order steak. See there.'

Kelvin looked at the relevant calligraphy which could have

been Greek to him, if it hadn't already been Chinese. 'Good. Well, where is it, then?'

The waiter looked carefully up and down the table. There was definitely no steak to be seen. 'I order steak so you must have eaten it already.'

'Don't be daft,' said Kelvin. 'You've only just brought my plate. How could I have possibly had time to eat it? I haven't even dirtied my fork yet.'

The waiter picked up Kelvin's fork and took it over to the window where he held it up to the light and carefully examined it. He returned. 'So you eat steak with your fingers.'

The rest of us were now agog. It was a lovely conversation to listen in to.

Kelvin, remarkably, was holding on to his temper. He seemed to be more baffled than angry. He shifted uneasily in his chair. 'Look. If you want your bill to be paid, just stop messing about and go and get me my steak.'

That was a threat that will cow waiters the world over. Ours scurried back behind the bar and engaged in a bellowed conversation with the guardian of the hatch. It did not seem to satisfy him and he came back with an aggressive glint in his eye. 'Cook say he give you steak.'

'Well, Cook's got it bloody well wrong!' said Kelvin in exasperation.

'He didn't get his steak, you know,' said Lindy. The majority of the meal was now distributed and we could afford to join in.

The waiter looked round at us, his eyes peering at each of us in turn. 'You all say he not got steak?'

'Yes!' we chorused.

'You all not pay for steak?'

'We all not pay for steak,' agreed the commander.

'Excuse me,' said the waiter and he withdrew back to the hatch where a furious altercation ensued.

'He seems to be remarkably scrutable for his race,' observed Dennis.

There was a crash as the hatch was slammed shut and a door beside the bar flew open. We turned to see what the fuss was about and observed a Chinese wearing a white apron and overalls burst into the restaurant waving his arms around and shouting at the waiter. The waiter pointed out Kelvin and shouted back. They both came over to the table.

'You're on your own, Kelvin,' murmured Lindy.

The cook stopped by Kelvin and stabbed his finger at the plate. 'Omelette,' he hissed.

'Yes,' agreed Kelvin cautiously.

The chef grasped the omelette in both hands and pulled. It was a bit like a conjuring trick. The egg peeled away to reveal a steak nestling inside. 'Steak, bloody steak. You see bloody steak, yes? Steak omelette, what waiter man ask for.'

The waiter burst into impassioned speech which cannot have been polite as the chef struck him a clumsy blow on the chest. The waiter retaliated and this drew forth a shriek of fury from the chef who chased the waiter round the table and pursued him into the kitchen where bangs and crashes revealed that the disagreement was continuing.

'They can get a bit excited, these people,' observed the commander.

Kelvin was looking sadly at his steak omelette. 'I don't think I want it now,' he said. 'Not after that chap has fingered it.'

'I wouldn't worry,' said Mary. 'He was the chef, after all. He's bound to have fingered everything.'

'That's not the same. He fingered it in public. And there's a dirty great thumbprint in the middle of the steak.'

'Bad luck,' said Dennis, thoughtfully examining a wrinkled brown object that he had speared with his fork. 'I've no idea what this is, but it's really rather good.'

With the waiter out of the restaurant and, judging by the noise, likely to be absent for a while, the businessmen began to fold their newspapers and tiptoe away. Kelvin shovelled his mangled steak omelette on to a side-plate and began to tour the remains of the other dishes. The commander saw him coming and snatched up the last two morsels of lemon chicken. Frustrated and hungry, Kelvin returned to his omelette, deciding to pick at the bits untouched by human hand.

The waiter eventually re-emerged and toured the tables

vacated by the businessmen, harvesting pound notes and piles of luncheon vouchers before coming to our table and handing the bill to Kelvin who was just mopping up the last remaining morsel on his plate. Some of the starch had been knocked out of the waiter, a button was missing from his white jacket and he carried a napkin in front of his mouth. The bill was extremely modest and the commander took it and carefully added it up.

'He hasn't charged you for the steak omelette.'

'I no charge for steak omelette. Bloody chef mess it up. It is on the house.'

'Oh, I see,' said the commander. 'That is very generous.'

'Thank you,' said the waiter, withdrawing. We divided the bill by six. There was a debate about the tip. Some felt that nothing was deserved under the circumstances, but the free steak omelette which Kelvin had eaten swayed the majority and 10 per cent was agreed upon. We laid down our money and left, waiting half-way down the stairs while Martha and the commander visited their respective loos.

'Interesting sort of meal, that,' observed Dennis.

'Yes,' said Mary. 'It was very different and surprisingly good. I think I might go to a Chinese restaurant again.'

Suddenly there was a scream from the floor above us. We craned our necks to see the waiter leaning over the bannisters and looking down at us. 'Ho!' he yelled and threw something down the central well of the staircase towards us. We instinctively ducked, but Mary was struck on the head. It was three screwed-up pound notes. 'I don't want tip. Bloody cook gives you steak omelette. That is bad. I only take tips when the job is good.' He turned away leaving us gazing, dumbfounded, after him.

'Heavens!' said Dennis. 'A waiter refusing a tip! The earth must have wobbled on its axis.'

'Look out!' said Mary. 'He's back.'

The waiter was leaning over the bannisters again, the napkin still covering his nose. 'You are stupid, stupid people!' he yelled.

Dennis waved and smiled at him. 'Hullo, hullo, thank you very much.'

'What are you doing?' asked Mary.

'Humouring him. I've read about these orientals. They can run amok if you don't keep them sweet.'

'What's amok?' asked Kelvin.

'They pick up an axe and rush about chopping people up until somebody kills them. I think it's the Chinese who do it. Or it may be the Malays.' Judging by the sudden burst of foreign tongues above us, the chef had joined the waiter and the amok was about to take place.

'Shall we wait outside for the others?' suggested Mary.

'I think that might be the wisest course,' agreed Dennis, and we all scuttled down the rest of the stairs to wait in the street for the commander and Martha.

'I'm not sure I'd go to another Chinese restaurant,' said Kelvin. 'I thought they behaved rather strangely.' There was nobody to say, 'They're not all like that,' because for all we knew they probably were.

'Let's go and see Shakespeare's birthplace,' said Martha.

'How long before the play starts?' asked Lindy.

'Five and a half hours,' was the grim response.

We strolled across the town, gently burping up our bean sprouts like cows savouring the cud, towards the hallowed birthplace of the bard. It seemed to be very suburban as we approached.

'That's handy,' remarked Mary, 'he was born just up the road from the library. I bet that's what made him decide to be a writer.'

There was an entry charge so we did not go in but trailed back towards the town centre.

'I could have gone out hunting today,' said Mary.

'You can go out hunting every day, but it's not every day that you have the opportunity to see a great play,' replied Dennis.

'Do you really hunt?' asked Martha, as we scuffed through the great drifts of fallen leaves along the edge of the river.

'Yes. Two or three times a week usually.'

'Don't you feel a bit uncomfortable about it?'

'No, not really. One is used to it now. One's backside gets hardened quite quickly.'

'No, I don't mean that. I mean uncomfortable about the principle of hunting foxes. I think it's disgraceful that it still goes on in this day and age.'

'Hunting foxes? Oh no. I would never dream about going fox hunting. Dreadful pompous conceited lot who do, and they know nothing about the countryside.'

'That's good,' said Martha with relief. 'I find fox hunting indefensible.'

'So do I,' concurred Mary heartily. 'You spend your time sitting about in the freezing cold for hours beside a covert waiting for something to happen. I haven't done it for years. It bores me witless.'

'I suppose you drag hunt, then?'

'Heavens no! I go stag hunting. Much more fun. Better chase and a decent kill at the end of the day to show for it rather than a ratty scrap of red fur well chewed over by the hounds. You ought to come out with us for a day.'

'No, thank you,' said Martha faintly, as disturbed as only a *Guardian*-reading, liberal-arts college lecturer could be, confronted by one who flouted all the shibboleths so brazenly.

We entered the church where the bard was interred. A custodian seated in the chancel solicited a donation before we could go through to the grave.

'Is that all?' said Kelvin. 'It's not much to look at, is it? Just a bit of paving stone with a rope round it. You can't even read the writing on it.'

Martha was shocked. 'It's the grave of William Shakespeare.'

'I know that, but so what?'

'So what? You're standing a few yards from the skull that housed the brain of one of the greatest geniuses that the world has ever known.'

'Yes, but the skull's been vacant for a good while now and, personally, I'd rather read the fatstock prices than *Romeo and Juliet*.'

'You're just a boor, Kelvin,' said the commander, who was standing reverently to attention beside the steps that led to the grave and the altar.

'Is he just? Well, when did you last read anything by Shakespeare?' asked Lindy.

'Er . . . not for a bit.'

'Not since you left school, I'll bet. And what play was it that you last read?'

'*Antony and Cleopatra.*'

'Is that the one that had Sid James as Antony?' asked Kelvin.

'That's right, and Kenneth Williams played Caesar. It was quite funny,' replied the commander.

'I think that was a "Carry On" film,' said Dennis. 'It was Burton and Taylor who did the original.'

'Oh yes. Quite right,' said the commander.

Martha decided to educate us. 'That's probably the best likeness of Shakespeare that we have,' she said, indicating the bust high in its niche on the wall to the left of the grave.

We examined it critically. 'He looks a bit like a doctored cat,' said Kelvin.

'He does, doesn't he?' replied Dennis. 'I expect the chap who carved it wasn't very good.'

'Well, if he wasn't very good, how do we know that Shakespeare looked like that?' said Kelvin. 'It's like that chap with a squint who's a woodcarver up at the commune. He keeps doing busts of people that always end up looking like monkeys.'

'We have other portraits,' said Martha. 'Like the ones we would have seen back at the birthplace.'

'When were they done?' asked Dennis.

'I suppose the earliest was produced about twenty years after his death.'

'I bet they just copied that ratty little carving up there. For all we know, Shakespeare may have had one eye and his nose spread over his face.'

Kelvin, having spread scorn over one of our national shrines, stumped back to one of the pews and ostentatiously pulled out a copy of *Farmers Weekly* from the enormous poacher's pocket built into his jacket, put on his reading glasses, licked his fingers and began to study the aforementioned fatstock prices. Dennis slipped out of the chancel to join him and persuaded him to turn to the crossword in which they became absorbed.

The mourners round the grave became restive. 'How long until the play starts?' asked Mary.

'Four hours,' replied Martha.

'What can we do now?' asked the commander.

'I know what I'd like to do,' said Mary. 'I'd like to have a go on that organ.'

We looked at her in surprise. 'I didn't know you could play,' said Lindy.

'I quite often play in chapel on Sunday, but I've never managed to play on an instrument as good as that.' 'That' was a great bank of pipes stuck above the aisle with a small playing booth to the right of the pulpit.

'I didn't know you went to chapel,' said Lindy.

'Yes. I enjoy playing on the organ.'

Religion was a subject that was largely avoided in our community because the diversity of beliefs could have led to serious disagreements. We had a few recusants whose needs were ministered to by a decrepit priest who fancied himself as an intellectual theologian. There was the C. of E. but it had never recovered from the excesses of its clergy a century ago when they had had a whale of a time drinking, hunting and whoring, leaving the souls of their parishioners as easy pickings for Wesley and a host of evangelical imitators who left their places of worship scattered along the lanes, as common as Dutch barns. If you weren't established, you tended to worship at the nearest chapel dedicated to some obscure Old Testament figure or other and hope that transgression of the fundamental stricture that was common to all of them – never to let a drop of alcohol pass between your lips – might be forgiven on the day of judgement.

Mary moved hungrily towards the organ and rattled at the door that kept casual fingers away from its keys.

'I'd leave it alone,' said Martha nervously, looking round the interior of the church. The guardian of Shakespeare's tomb seemed half-asleep and unlikely to object, but there were a couple of semi-official Women's Institute types peddling *memento mori* at the entrance of the church and they were looking at Kelvin and Dennis with some disapproval. Dennis had taken over the crossword while Kelvin had stretched himself out along the pew for a quick nap.

'Don't be silly,' said Mary. 'What's an organ for if it's not to be played? Commander!' Like Kelvin's whistle in the restaurant, Mary's voice had been evolved to control hounds during the bedlam of the kill and to summon her husband from several fields away when he was riding the tractor in his earmuffs. It was probably the loudest noise, including the organ, to have pierced the dim religious quiet for centuries and the bust of the bard tottered on its perch. The commander hurried to her side. 'Commander, can you break into this organ?'

Mary, although she had lowered her voice, was clearly audible throughout the church. The WI ladies twittered to each other about whether they ought to interfere, but they were occupied by a large group of Japanese tourists who had entered and were hissing their way round the souvenirs. A few of them had decided to follow Kelvin's example and were now stretched along the pews with their eyes closed. They must have thought this was the western way of worship or how one showed respect to the tombs of famous forefathers.

The commander, with deft fingers that had probably unlocked the Polaris firing mechanisms, opened up the organ loft and, with Martha almost in tears at the lack of respect being shown by her charges, Mary switched on the lights and fiddled with the stops. There was a preliminary blare that woke the wondering children of Nippon and Mary was off in a rousing rendition of *D'ye ken John Peel?*.

Martha pulled Mary from the stool. 'For heaven's sake, if you must play, at least choose something more appropriate. This is a church, after all.'

'Oh very well,' said Mary. 'What do you suggest?'

'How about *Eternal Father Strong to Save*?' suggested the commander.

'Right.' Mary pulled out all the stops and let it rip. She and the commander bellowed out the accompaniment while Martha retreated to the back of the church to dissociate herself from them. In consideration of the nature of the

congregation, Mary then switched to selections from *The Mikado* and Kelvin, mindful of the amount of money that the Grabber sometimes came to the pub with, rousted out the guardian of the chancel, who was quite enjoying the concert, and the two of them went amidst the tourists with a collection plate. They made enough to pay for the complete refurbishment of the bust in luminous paint, with sufficient over to re-carve the bardic slab.

We wandered back to the town in a pleasantly mellow mood. Dennis had finished his crossword and all, save Martha, had thoroughly enjoyed *The Mikado* and the few excerpts from *Madame Butterfly* which had been the encore when it was discovered how generous the tourists had been in donating to church funds.

We had tea in a shoppe, mooched round a bookshop and peered over the wall at the son or the grandson of the sacred tree under which the bard was wont to sit, eventually gravitating to the Memorial Theatre to sit in the relentlessly stylish cafe where we played 'Animal, vegetable and mineral' to while away the time. As 7.30 approached, the cafe began to fill with people, mainly with scores of children.

'It's not a kiddies' play, is it?' asked Kelvin.

'Oh no,' replied Martha. 'They're all probably doing it for "O" or "A" level this year. Any Shakespeare play you go to has an audience that is full of young people.'

'Does the theatre make a profit?' asked Mary.

'No, the Arts Council and all sorts of other organizations have to subsidize it. But I believe Stratford is closer to break-even point than most theatres that put on Shakespeare.'

Kelvin was puzzled. 'But if it doesn't make a profit, why don't they put on plays that people want to see?'

Martha was shocked. 'This is the Shakespeare Memorial Theatre. It has to stage Shakespeare. His plays are part of our national culture.'

'It seems a bit daft to me. If it wasn't for all these kids, there'd be nobody here and they're only here because they're forced to be. I reckon this Shakespeare has only survived because of the bloody examiners making people do him at school.'

Our seats were up in the gods, or should have been. The gods were crammed by shrieking teenagers pinching each other's bottoms, hitting each other with programmes and hurling peanuts across the aisle. It looked as though the atmosphere of the Colosseum would be effortlessly achieved. Martha stayed there to keep an eye on her pupils, but none of the rest of us was prepared to endure the vertigo brought on by looking down the precipitous slope of tiered seats, bristling with punk haircuts, towards the tiny stage far below.

As the curtain rose, so did we, clattering our way down the steps from the upper circle that led to the street outside. Back in through the main entrance we went, where we bluffed our way past the attendants into the stalls. It was both more peaceful and more comfortable there, and we settled down to look at the stage.

'I thought this was supposed to be *Julius Caesar*,' said Kelvin.

'So did I,' said Dennis, leaning over to look at the programme belonging to an American in the row in front. It had been decided that quite enough had been spent without buying fripperies like programmes. 'It is.'

'But it can't be. Bugger me, it is! That fat chap has just said something about a holiday to see Caesar.'

There were people saying 'shhh' in a variety of foreign tongues all round us.

'But Romans are supposed to wear things like bedsheets,' persisted Kelvin.

'Togas,' said Dennis.

'That's right. But this lot are wearing brown uniforms and jackboots. They surely never wore gear like that.'

'Perhaps they can't afford to buy the right sort of costume,' suggested Dennis.

'I think it's a bloody disgrace,' said Mary. 'When we did *The Mikado*, it was no trouble to ask people to make up their own costumes. They could have at least done the same. And look at that photograph.' The stage was dominated by a huge photograph of a face, presumably of Caesar himself. 'They didn't have photos in those days. It's ridiculous.'

We sat there in silence for a bit, seething with discontent.

'Can you make out what they're saying?' asked Dennis.

'Not very well,' said Kelvin. He cupped his hands and yelled across the hallowed air towards the stage, 'Speak up!'

The commander and I could take no more of this and moved several rows further back. Caesar himself had arrived on stage and strode about saying 'ha' and 'ho' for a bit until the soothsayer arrived. There were snorts of delight from the groundlings in front of us.

'He's the spitting image of Jimmy,' announced Kelvin loudly. One of the usherettes came down to read the riot act and an uneasy peace descended until Caesar and his entourage arrived on stage bizarrely decked in gold polythene. 'I bet they got these costumes from a job lot of *Dr Who* stuff,' said Kelvin very audibly, and received an appropriately dagger-like glare from Brutus across the footlights. 'What the hell's that noise meant to be?' A most curious tweeting sound

was echoing around the theatre, which a discussion among the rustics eventually identified as the sound of scores of electronic watches all deciding that it was 8.00 pm at roughly the same moment.

It was not really the play that we should have gone to see. Kelvin went to sleep after his TV star had had her moment on stage and revealed quite a lot of thigh for quite a long time while she was showing her scars. He slept through thunderstorm, assassination and Mark Antony's speech and only the electric excitement generated by Dennis at the prospect of having a drink, brought him, snorting, out of his doze just before the interval.

Afterwards, Mary and Dennis both joined him in sleep. Even Martha agreed later that they had not missed all that much. The most memorable, if embarrassing, moment of the production took place when Brutus committed hara-kiri. He pounced on his sword with an enthusiasm weirdly akin to the way that Kelvin would have jumped on Matilda, had he ever had the chance. There was a moment of stunned silence before the gods erupted in laughter which spread as far as the stalls.

We did not get home until 2.00 am, but it was generally agreed that it had been worth going. Mary got the producer's job in *Blithe Spirit* on the strength of it. Dennis was asked to speak to four WIs on the experience and Kelvin bored the local pub about it for weeks. There is some talk about booking a coach to go to see *No Sex, Please, We're British* next year.